JavaScript

Cheat Sheet

(Cover all Basic
JavaScript Syntaxes)

Ray Yao

About This Book

This book covers all basic JavaScript syntaxes, almost each syntax entry lists a program example and result output. We can quickly reference the most helpful programming syntaxes, such as common command syntax, string function syntax, collection function syntax, class & object syntax......; all these syntaxes are very useful for programming.

We can take this book as a basic syntax manual because its entries are arranged alphabetically so that we can easily reference the important syntax.

Nowadays or in the future, the JavaScript Syntax Book can provide great help for coding both in our study and our work.

Copyright © 2015 by Ray Yao's Team, All Rights Reserved

Disclaimer

This book is intended as a basic syntax manual only; it cannot include all entries on this subject. Its purpose is as a supplement for a cheat sheet book, not as a whole JavaScript dictionary.

Table of Contents

4

6

Syntax Chart

<script>

......

</script>

// "<script>......</script>" is a tag for JavaScript. The JavaScript codes are included within it.

// We can also use "<script type = "text/javascript">...</script>".

// We can also use "<script language="javascript">...</script>".

e.g.

<script>

document.write("Hello World!");

</script>

// Output: Hello World!

$ syntax:

var $ = value;   // "$" can be treated as a letter

let $ = value;   // "$" can be treated as a letter

// $$ can be treated as two letters,

// $$$ can be treated as three letters.

e.g.

<script>

let $ =100; let $$ = 200;   // define two variables

document.write($ + $$);

</script>

// Output: 300

? : operator syntax:

(test-expression) ? (if-true-do-this) : (if-false-do-this);

```
// if (test-expression) returns true, run (if-true-do-this)

// if (test-expression) returns false, run (if-false-do-this)

e.g.

<script>

var x=100; var y=200;

var result = (x < y) ? "apple" : "banana";

// (test-expression) ? (if-true-do-this) : (if-false-do-this);

 document.write ( result );

</script>

// Output:   apple
```

?? syntax:

argument1 ?? argument2;

```
// Return the first argument if the first argument is not null or undefined.

// Return the second argument if the first argument is null or undefined.

e.g.

<script>

var fruit1 = null;

var fruit2 = "Apple";

var fruit = fruit1 ?? fruit2;

document.write("My favorite fruit is " + fruit);

</script>

// Output:   My favorite fruit is Apple
```

=== syntax:

variable1 === variable2

```
// Return true if the type and value of variable1 is equal to the type and
value of variable2. Otherwise return false.

e.g.

<script>
```

```
var x = "Hello"; var y = "Hello";

document.write( x === y );

</script>
```

// Output: true

/   /g syntax:

/regular expression/g

// Return all items that matches the regular expression

// "g" means global search.

e.g.

```
<script>

var str="What day is today?";

var patt=/day/g;

document.write(str.match(patt));

</script>
```

// Output: day, day

/   /i syntax:

/regular expression/i

// Return an index of the item that matches the regular expression.

// "i" means case insensitive.

e.g.

```
<script>

var str = "Visual Basic";

var position = str.search(/basic/i);   // return the index

document.write(position);

</script>
```

// Output: 7

/   /m syntax:

/regular expression/m

// Perform a match in multiline string

// "m" means multiline search

e.g.

```
<script>
let text = "In the afternoon, \n we play football in the playground";
let result = text.match( /in/m );   /* Make a multiline search for "in" in
each line of a string. */
document.write("Result is: " + result);
</script>
```

// Output: Result is: in

----

variable1 !== variable2

// Return true if the type or value of variable1 is not equal to the type or
value of variable2. Otherwise return false.

e.g.

```
<script>
var x = "Hi"; var y = "Hello";
document.write( x !== y );
</script>
```

// Output: true

"+" strings syntax:

str = str1 + str2;

// "+" operators can connect two strings together.

e.g.

```
<script>
s1="JavaScript "; s2=" is very easy!";
str = s1 + s2;
document.write(str);
```

```
</script>
```

// Output: JavaScript is very easy!

----

abs() syntax:

Math.abs(number)

// Math.abs( ) returns an absolute value of a number.

e.g.

```
<script>

var num = Math.abs( -100 );

document.write( num + " ");

</script>
```

// Output: 100

----

acos() syntax:

Math.acos(number)

// Return the arccosine (radians) of a number.

// The parameter number is expected between -1 and 1.

e.g.

```
<script>

document.write(Math.acos(0.5));

</script>
```

// Output: 1.0471975511965979

----

add() syntax:

set.add(value)

// Add a value to a Set

e.g.

```
<script>

const mySet = new Set();    // create a Set

mySet.add("a");    // add values to the mySet
```

```
mySet.add("b");

mySet.add("c");

document.write(mySet.size);     // show the size of mySet

</script>

// Output:   3
```

----

addEventListener() syntax:

```
document.getElementById("Btn").addEventListener("click",
function(){});

// Add event listener to the specified element

e.g.

<html>

<button id="Btn">Click</button>

<script>

document.getElementById("Btn").addEventListener("click",
function(){ alert("Hi, My friends!");});

</script>

</html>

// Output:   Hi, My friends!
```

----

alert() syntax:

```
alert(contents);

// pops up a message and show the specified contents

e.g.

<script language="javascript">

alert("Hello World!");     // pop up a message

</script>

// Output:   Hello World!
```

----

anchors syntax:

document.anchors

// "anchors" means <a></a> element.

e.g.

<html>

<a name = "A">Ruby</a>

<a name = "B">Rust</a>

<a name = "C">Perl</a>

<script>

let size = **document.anchors.length;**   // get <a></a> size

document.write("The number of 'a' element is: " + size);

</script>

</html>

// Output:

Ruby

Rust

Perl

The number of 'a' element is: 3

----

anonymous function syntax:

var handle = function(args) { return value };

// Anonymous function has no function name, it is called by a handle

e.g.

<script>

var handle = **function (a, b) {return a + b};**   // anonymous function

document.write(handle(10, 20));

</script>

// Output: 30

----

appCodeName syntax:

let browser = navigator.appCodeName;

// Get the code name of the browser

// Note: "navigator" may return an inaccurate information.

e.g.

<script>

let browser = navigator.appCodeName;

document.write("Browser code name is : " + browser);

</script>

// Output: Browser code name is : Mozilla

----

appendChild() syntax:

window.document.createElement( );

appendClild( );

// "window.document.createElement( )" creates an element with the specified name.

// "appendClild( )" appends an element as a last child element.

e.g.

<html>

<script>

var myLine = document.createElement("hr");

// creates an element "hr", a horizontal ruled line tag

document.body.appendChild(myLine);

// appends a child element "myLine" to the html body

</script>

</html>

// Output: _____

----

apply() syntax:

function.apply(this, array);

// Call a function, the first argument must be the object itself.

e.g.

```
<script>

function myFun(x, y) { return x + y;}

var myArr = [10, 20]

var myObj = myFun.apply(this, myArr);   // call myFun()

document.write(myObj);

</script>

// Output:   30
```

----

apply() syntax:

function.apply(arrayObj);

// Call s function with a specified array object.

// It can be applied to different array object.

e.g.

```
<script>

var student = {

info: function() {    // define a function

return this.name + "  " + this.class;

}}

var stud1 = { name:"Andy", class: "Class 1", }   // array

var stud2 = { name:"Betty", class: "Class 2", }   // array

var detail = student.info.apply(stud2);   // call info:function()

// show detail about the student2

document.write( detail );

</script>

// Output:  Betty Class 2
```

----

appName syntax:

let browser = navigator.appName;

// Get browser name

22

// Note: "navigator" may return an inaccurate information.

e.g.

\<script\>

let browser = navigator.appName;

document.write("Browser Name is : " + browser);

\</script\>

// Output: Browser Name is : Netscape

----

appVersion syntax:

let version = navigator.appVersion;

// Get browser version

// Note: "navigator" may return an inaccurate information.

e.g.

\<script\>

let version = navigator.appVersion;

document.write("Browser version is : " + version);

\</script\>

// Output: Browser version is : 5.0 (Windows NT 6.3; WOW64)

AppleWebKit/537.36 (KHTML, like Gecko) Chrome......

----

arguments object syntax:

arguments[index]

// "arguments" object can access the function arguments

e.g.

\<script\>

myFun(10, 11, 12, 13, 14, 15);

function myFun() {document.write(**arguments[2]**);}

\</script\>

// Output: 12

----

var array-name = new Array ("value0", "value1", "value2");

// An array is a particular variable, which can contain one or more value at a time. new Array( ) creates an array.

e.g.

```
<script>
var arr = new Array ("A", "B", "C");
document.write(arr[0], arr[1], arr[2]);
</script>
```

// Output: ABC

----

array creating syntax:

var array-name = new Array ( );

array-name[index0] = "value1";

array-name[index1] = "value1";

array-name[index2] = "value2";

// An array is a particular variable, which can contain one or more value at a time. new Array( ) creates an array.

e.g.

```
<script>
var color = new Array ( );    // create an array
color[0] = " red ";  color[1] = " yellow ";  color[2] = " green ";
document.write( color[0], color[1], color[2]);
</script>
```

// Output: red yellow green

----

array length syntax:

array.length

// Get the length of an array

e.g.

```
<script>
var color = new Array("yellow", "purple", "orange");
var size = color.length;     // get the size of an array
document.write ( size );
</script>
// Output:   3
```

----

arrow function syntax:

let functionName = (argument) => { return value };

// The arrow function is more concise than that of ordinary function.

e.g.

```
<script>
const myFun = (x, y) => { return x + y };
document.write(myFun(100, 200));
</script>
// Output:   300
```

----

asin() syntax:

Math.asin(number);

// Return the arcsine (radians) of a number.

// The parameter number is expected between -1 and 1.

e.g.

```
<script>
document.write( Math.asin(0.5));
</script>
// Output:   0.5235987755982989
```

----

atan() syntax:

Math.atan(number);

// Return the arctangent value of a number between -PI/2 and PI/2 radians.

e.g.

```
<script>

document.write ( Math.atan(1));

</script>
```

// Output: 0.7853981633974483

----

availHeight syntax:

screen.availHeight;

// Return the height of the screen

e.g.

```
<script>

height = screen.availHeight;

document.write( "Current screen height is " + height + "px");

</script>
```

// Output: Current screen height is 738px

----

availWidth syntax:

screen.availWidth;

// Return the width of the screen

e.g.

```
<script>

width = screen.availWidth;

document.write( "Current screen width is " + width + "px");

</script>
```

// Output: Current screen width is 1024px

----

back() syntax:

window.history.back()

// Go back to the previous web page in the history

e.g.

```html
<html>
<button onclick="history.back()">Go Back</button>
</html>
```

// Result: Go back to the previous page

----

blur() syntax:

element.blur()

// Remove focus from an element

e.g.

```html
<html>
<input type="text" id="tf" value="text field"><br>
<button type="button" onclick="removeFocus()">Remove Focus</button>
<script>
function removeFocus() {
document.getElementById("tf").blur();
}
</script>
</html>
```

// Result: The focus is removed when the button is clicked.

Boolean() syntax:

Boolean(test_expression)

// Check if the test_expression returns true

e.g.

```html
<script>
document.write(Boolean(100 > 10));
</script>
```

// Output: true

---

if (condition) break;

// "break" keyword is used to stop running the loop according to the condition.

e.g.

```
<script>

var num=0;

while (num<10) {

if (num==5) break;     // exit the "while loop" if num is 5

num++;

}

document.write ( num );

</script>
```

// Output: 5

---

function.call(this, argument);

// Call a function, the first argument must be the object itself.

e.g.

```
<script>

function sum(x, y) { return x + y; }

var myObj = sum.call( this, 10, 20 );  // calling sum() function

document.write(myObj);

</script>
```

// Output: 30

Math.ceil(argument);

// "Math.ceil( );" returns a closest integer that is greater than or equal to its argument.

e.g.

<script>

var num = 9.5;

document.write ("Ceiling number is "+**Math.ceil(num)**);

</script>

// Output: Ceiling number is 10

----

charAt() syntax:

string.charAt(number)

// "string.charAt(number)" can find a character in a string.

// "number" is an index of the string, beginning with 0.

e.g.

<script>

var mystring = "JavaScript is easy";

var ch = **mystring.charAt (2);**

// search a character at index 2

document.write (ch);

</script>

// Output: v

----

charCodeAt() syntax:

string.charCodeAt(index)

// Return Unicode code of a letter at the specified position.

e.g.

<script>

var str = "Hello world!";

var u = **str.charCodeAt(4);**   // return unicode

document.write ("The character's unicode at index 4 is " + u);

</script>

// Output:

The character's unicode at index 4 is 111

----

checkbox syntax:

<input type="checkbox" id= "ID value= "myValue">

// A group of checkboxes allows multiple boxes to be checked at any time and submit the selected value to handle.

e.g.

```
<html><body>

<form name="myform">

<input type= "checkbox"  id="color" value= "Red" onClick=
"myfun(this.value )"/> Red

<input type= "checkbox"  id="color" value= "Yellow" onClick=
"myfun(this.value )"/> Yellow

<input type= "checkbox"  id="color" value= "Green" onClick=
"myfun(this.value )"/> Green

</form>

<script>

function myfun( v) {

alert ( "You select:  " + v );

}     // assume that we select Red checkbox

</script>

</body></html>
```

// Output: You select: Red

----

checkValidity() syntax:

input.checkValidity() == true/false

// Return true if the data in the input element is valid, False otherwise.

input.validationMessage

// "input.validationMessage" will show the validity message.

30

e.g.

```html
<html>
<input id="fm" type="number" min="100" max="300" required>
<button onclick="myFun()">Check</button>
<script>
function myFun() {  // please input a number between 100 and 300
var num = document.getElementById("fm");
if (num.checkValidity() == false) {
document.write(num.validationMessage);
} else {
document.write("Correct Input");
}}
</script>
</html>
// Output:   Correct Input
```

----

childNodes syntax:

const nodeList = document.body.childNodes;

// Return a node list, the first child node is list[0], the second child node is list[1], ….

e.g.

```html
<html>
<p>Text A</p>
<p>Text B</p>
<script>
const list = document.body.childNodes;
document.write("The first childnode is: ")
document.write(list[0].nodeName);
</script>
</html>
```

```
// Output:
Text A
Text B
The first childnode is: P
```

---

class & method syntax:

```
class ClassName {      // create a class
  method1() { ... }     // define method1
  method2() { ... }     // define method2
}
// Class is a template for JavaScript objects.
e.g.
<script>
class Person {     // create a class
  read() {     // define a method
    document.write("I am reading a book!");
  }
}
let student = new Person();     // create an object
student.read();     // call the method
</script>
// Output:   I am writing a book!
```

---

class & property syntax:

```
class ClassName {      // create a class
  constructor(arg1, arg2) {     // define a constructor
    this.property1 = arg1;     // define property1
    this.property2 = arg2; }     // define property2
}
// Class is a template for JavaScript objects.
```

e.g.

```
<script>
class Person {    // create a class
  constructor(firstname, lastname) {
    this.firstname = firstname;    // proerty1
    this.lastname = lastname;      // proerty2
 }}
let author = new Person("Ray", "Yao");    // create an object
document.write(
author.firstname + " " + author.lastname );
</script>
// Output:  Ray Yao
```

----

clearInterval() syntax:

clearInterval(intervalVariable)

// "clearInterval()" clears the timer set with the setInterval() method

e.g.

```
<html>
<button onclick="stopFun()">Stop</button>
<p id="study"></p>
<script>
var intervalVar=setInterval(function(){myClock()},1000);
function myClock(){
var now=new Date();
var t=now.toLocaleTimeString();
document.getElementById("study").innerHTML=t;
}    // please click the "Stop" button
function stopFun(){clearInterval(intervalVar);}
</script>
</html>
```

33

9:26:18 PM

----

cleartimeout() syntax:

clearTimeout(timeoutVar);

// "clearTimeout()" clears the timer set with the setTimeOut() method

e.g.

```
<html>
<p id="study"></p>
<button onclick="stopFun()">Stop</button>
<script>  // Please click the Stop button within 3 seconds!
const timer = setTimeout(message, 3000);
function message() {
  document.getElementById("study").innerHTML = "You can see this
message because you forgot clicking the 'Stop' button within 3
seconds!"
}
function stopFun() {
document.write("Thank you for clicking the 'Stop' button within 3
seconds!");
  clearTimeout(timer);
}
</script>
</html>
```

// Output:

Stop

Thank you for clicking the 'Stop' button within 3 seconds!

----

window.close( );

// "window.close( );" can close the current window.

e.g.

```
<script>
function shut(){
alert("The window will be closed!")
window.close( );    // close the current window
}
</script>
<form>
<input type = "button" onclick = "shut()"  value = "Close">
</form>
```

// Result: The window is closed when the button is clicked

----

comment syntax:

//   This is a single line comment

/* This is a multi line comment; JavaScript interpreter will ignore both single line comment and multi line comment. ***/**

e.g.

```
<script type = "text/javascript">
document.write ("Hello World");    // show "Hello World".
/* "document.write()" shows the content "Hello World". "document.write (
)" is usually used to display the specified contents to users  */
</script>
```

// Output: Hello World

----

concat() syntax:

string1.concat(string2)

// Connect two strings together

35

e.g.

```
<script>
var str1 = "Hello! "
var str2 = "My friend.";
var result = str1.concat ( str2 );    // connect two strings
document.write ( result );
</script>
// Output:   Hello!  My friend.
```

----

concat() syntax:

const arr = arr1.concat(arr2);

// Connect all elements of two arrays together

e.g.

```
<script>
const arr1 = ["A", "B", "C"];
const arr2 = ["D", "E", "F"];
const arr = arr1.concat(arr2);
document.write(arr);
</script>
// Output:    A,B,C,D,E,F
```

----

conditional operator syntax:

(test-expression) ? (if-true-do-this) : (if-false-do-this);

// if (test-expression) returns true, run (if-true-do-this)

// if (test-expression) returns false, run (if-false-do-this)

e.g.

```
<script>
var x=100; var y=200;
var result = (x < y) ? "apple" : "banana";
// (test-expression) ? (if-true-do-this) : (if-false-do-this);
```

document.write (result);

</script>

// Output: apple

----

confirm() syntax:

window.confirm( );

// Require user to confirm in a dialog box.

// When "OK" is clicked, return true in scripting.

// When "Cancel" is clicked, return false in scripting.

e.g.

<script>

var ask = **window.confirm("Are you sure?");**

// confirm() will return true or false

if (ask == true) { document.write ("All Right!"); }

else { document.write ("Cancel!"); }

</script>

// Output: All Right!   Cancel!

----

connect string syntax:

string1 + string2 + string3 + string4 + string5......

// The "+" operator can join strings together.

e.g.

<script>

var str1 = "JavaScript ";

var str2 = "is ";

var str3 = "very easy! ";

document.write (**str1 + str2 + str3**);   // connect strings

</script>

// Output: JavaScript is very easy!

----

connect string syntax:

var text = "string1 ";

text += "string2";

// Using "+=" can connect two strings in different lines.

e.g.

\<script\>

var text = "Java ";

text += "Cheat Sheet!";

document.write(text);

\</script\>

// Output: Java Cheat Sheet!

----

console.log() syntax:

console.log(message);

// console.log() is used to output message to a web console for debugging purpose.

// To check the result: please run the program by Chrome browser > F12 > Console

e.g.

\<html\>

\<script\>

console.log("We are debugging the code!");

\</script\>

\</html\>

// Run program by a browser > F12 > Console

// Output: We are debugging the code!

----

const syntax:

const constant = value;

// "const" is used to define a constant, which cannot be redefined and reassigned value.

e.g.

```
<script>
const x = 100;  const y = 200;   // define two constants
document.write( x + y);
</script>
// Output:   300
```

----

constructor() syntax:

```
function Constructor_Name(arg1, arg2) {   // constructor
  this.property1 = arg1;
  this.property2 = arg2;
}
// Constructor is used to initialize the properties of an object
// Constructor name is the same as the class name.
```

e.g.

```
<script>
function Person(name, age) {  // constructor
  this.name = name;
  this.age = age;
}
const student = new Person("Andy", 16);  // create an object
document.write("The student is " + student.name +"<br>" );
document.write("The student is " + student.age +"<br>" );
</script>
// Output:
The student is Andy
The student is 16
```

----

continue syntax:

```
if ( condition )  continue;
```

// "continue" keyword is used to stop the current iteration, ignoring the subsequent code, and then continue the next loop.

e.g.

```
<script>
var num=0;
while (num<10){
num++;
if (num==5) continue;     // go the next "while loop"
document.write(num);     // skip this if num is 5
}
</script>
// Output:   1234678910
// Note that the output has no 5.
```

----

cookie reading syntax:

var cookies = document.cookie;

// Get all cookies from browser.

// We need to use split() function to break all cookie strings into name and value pairs.

e.g.

```
<html>
<script>
function GetCookie() {
let myCookies = document.cookie;     // get cookies
document.write ("All Cookies : " + myCookies );
cookieArr = myCookies.split(';');
// break cookie strings into names and values
for(var n=0; n<cookieArr.length; n++) {
 // get name and value pair from cookie array
name = cookieArr[n].split('=')[0];
```

40

```
value = cookieArr[n].split('=')[1];

document.write ("Name is : " + name + " and Value is : " + value);

}}    // show all cookies in name and value pairs

 </script>

 <form name>

<input type = "button" value = "Get Cookie" onclick = "GetCookie()"/>

</form>

</html>
```

// Output: All Cookies : Name=; name=;

_ga=GA1.2.2124459580.1663288560;

_pbjs_userid_consent_data=6683316680106290;

_lr_env_src_ats=false;

__gads=ID=773395b32fdcd21f:T=1663288559:S=ALNI_MZSv2inauSa

VRD2QvdayYP6R4Q63w;

_cc_id=84de3d078c7676826eba0ae2c82e28b4;

panoramaId_expiry=1663893362710;......

----

cookie removing syntax:

document.cookie = "name=; expires=pastDate; path=/;";

// We just set the expires parameter to a past date, then the cookie will
be removed.

// "path" means the cookie path.

e.g.

document.cookie = "name=Andy; expires=**Thu, 01 Jan 1970 00:00:00
GMT**; path=/";

// Note: We need to specify the cookie path to make sure that we will
delete the right cookie.

----

cookie writing syntax:

document.cookie="name1=value1; name2=value2; expires=date";

// Set the cookie name, value, and expire date.

// Cookies are stored as name and value pairs.

```
<html>
<script>
function setCookie() {
var cookievalue = document.myform.user.value;
document.cookie = "name=; expires=Thu, 01 Jan 2800 00:00:00
GMT";    // set cookie
document.write ("Cookie Writing: Name = " + cookievalue + ";");}
</script>
<form name = "myform" >
Enter cookie <input type = "text" name = "user"/>
<input type = "button" value = "Set Cookie" onclick = "setCookie();"/>
</form>
</html>
```

// Output: Cookie Writing: Name = Ray Yao;

----

cos() syntax:

Math.cos(radian)

// Return the cosine value of a radian.

e.g.

```
<script>
document.write(Math.cos(3.14).toFixed(2));
</script>
```

// Output: -1.00

----

createElement( ) syntax:

window.document.createElement( );

appendClild( );

// "window.document.createElement( )" creates an element with the specified name.

// "appendClild( )" appends an element as a last child element.

e.g.

<html>

<script>

var myLine = document.createElement("hr");

// creates an element "hr", a horizontal ruled line tag

document.body.appendChild(myLine);

// appends a child element "myLine" to the html body

</script>

</html>

// Output: _____

----

createTextNode() syntax:

window.document.createTextNode( );

appendChild( );

// "window.document.createTextNode( )" creates a text node with the specified text.

// "appendClild( )" appends a node as the last child node.

e.g.

<html><body>

<script>

var myText = document.createTextNode("Hello Dom!");

// creates a text node named "myText"

document.body.appendChild(myText);

// appends the text node "myText" to the html body

</script>

</body></html>

// Output: Hello Dom!

43

string – a character or a string of characters

number – an integer or floating point number

boolean – a value with true or false.

function – a user-defined method

object – a built-in or user-defined object

e.g.

var mystring="I am a string"; // mystring data type is a string.

var myinteger=168;   // myinteger data type is a number.

var myfloat=12.88;   // myfloat data type is a number.

var mybool=true;   // mybool data type is boolean.

// Note: String is always enclosed by a pair of double quotes.

----

var dateObject = new Date( )   // create a date object

// When using date and time, we must create a date object first.

e.g.

```
<script>
var dateObject = new Date( );   // create a date object
document.write ( dateObject );
</script>
```

// Output:

Thu Nov 05 2015 21:39:28 GMT-0500 (Eastern Time)

e.g.

```
<script>
const dateObj = new Date(2022, 0, 18, 22, 36, 28, 0);
document.write(dateObj);
</script>
```

// Output:

----

debugger syntax:

debugger;

// The debugger keyword stops running part of the JavaScript program. The debugger is use to set a break point.

// To check the result: please run the program by Chrome browser > F12 > Console……

// In the Console, if we press F5 to turn on the debugger, then the code below the "debugger;" will not run.

e.g.

```
<script>
document.write( "Please press F12, then click the Consol tag");
var result = 100 + 200;
console.log("If you press F5 to turn on the debugger, then you cannot see the following result 300.");
debugger;      // set break point
console.log(result);
</script>
```

// Output: Please press F12, then click the Consol tag

If you press F5 to turn on the debugger, then you cannot see the following result 300.

----

delete array element syntax:

delete array[index];

// Delete an array element according its index.

// After the element has been deleted, it will become "undefined"

e.g.

```
<script>
const letters = ["A", "B", "C", "D"];
document.write(
```

```
"The first letter is: " + letters[0] + "<br>");

delete letters[0];    // delete the array element

document.write(

"The first letter is: " + letters[0] + "<br>");

</script>

// Output:

The first letter is: A

The first letter is: undefined
```

----

delete() syntax:

map.delete(key);

// Delete a key/value pair according to the specified key in Map

e.g.

```
<script>

const myMap = new Map();

  myMap.set(1, " A");

  myMap.set(2, " B");

  myMap.set(3, " C");

myMap.delete(3);    // delete (3, "C")

document.write(myMap.size);

</script>

// Output:   2
```

----

do-while loop syntax:

do{ // some js code in here **} while (test-expression);**

// "do...while" loops through a block of code once, and then repeats the loop if the specified condition is true.

e.g.

```
<script>

var counter=0;
```

```
do {
document.write ( "@" );
counter++;     // increase 1 every loop
} while (counter<8);   // loop  8 times
</script>
// Output:  @@@@@@@@
```

----

document.write() syntax:

document.write(contents);

// show contents in web page

e.g

document.write("Hello World!");

// Output: Hello World!

----

dom element length syntax:

var collection = document.getElementsByTagName("tagName");

// "getElementsByTagName("tagName")" gets all elements by
"tagName", and return a collection.

conllection.length   // get the length of the collection

e.g.

```
<html>
<p>Text A</p>
<p>Text B</p>
<script>
var coll = document.getElementsByTagName("p");
document.write( "There are " + coll.length + " elements with tag
name P.");
</script>
</html>
```

// Output:

Text A

Text B

There are 2 elements with tag name P.

----

element value syntax

document.formName.elementName.value

// Get or set a value for the specified element.

e.g.

```
<html>

<form name="myForm">

<input type="text" name="myText" value="" />

<input type="submit" onClick="show()">

</form>

<script type="text/javascript">

function show(){
```

alert(**document.myForm.myText.value**);

// gets the value of data which the user has inputted

// Assume that we input "Hello World!"

```
}

</script>

</html>
```

// Output: Hello World!

----

endsWith() syntax:

string.endsWith(searchvalue, end)

// Return true if a string ends with a specified value

// The endsWith() method is case sensitive.

e.g.

```
<script>

var str = "HTML CSS is very easy";
```

document.write(str.**endsWith("easy")**);

</script>

// Output: true

----

entries() syntax:

const obj = arr.entries();

// "entries" returns an object with the array name/value pairs.

e.g.

<script>

const arr = [" Apple", " Banana", " Cherry"];

const obj = arr.entries();

for (let n of obj) {

document.write(n + "<br>");

}

</script>

// Output:

0, Apple

1, Banana

2, Cherry

----

eval() syntax:

eval(expression)

// Evaluate the expression. Please do not use eval() as possible, because it can run any code, and cause security problem.

e.g.

<script>

let x = 10; let y = 20;

let sum = **eval(x+y);**

document.write(sum);

</script>

// Output: 30

----

every() syntax:

array.every(callback_fucntion);

// "every()" checks if all element values meet a specified condition.

// Return true if all element values meet a specified condition.

e.g.

<script>

const arr = [10,20,30,40,50,60];

var num = **arr.every(myFun);**

document.write("Are all element values greater than 20 ? " + num);

function myFun(value) {

  return value > 20; // check if all element values are greater than 20

}

</script>

// Output: Are all element values greater than 20 ? false

----

exec() syntax:

pattern.exec("string");

// exec() searches character by using regular expression, return the character if the matched character is found, otherwise null.

e.g.

<script>

var patt=new RegExp("o");

document.write(patt.exec("Hello"));

</script>

// Output: o

----

export syntax:

export{ variable1, variable2, ……};

// Export the data to any files that need to import the data.

e.g.

const name = "Smith";

const age = 17;

export {name, age};

// Please save this file as "myExport.js", so that another file

"myImport.html" can import this file. (see the import syntax)

// The export file needs to work with the import file.

----

export default functionName;

// Export the data to any files that need to import the data.

e.g.

const person = () => {

const name = "Smith";

const age = 17;

return name + ' is ' + age + 'years old.';

};

export default person;

// Please save this file as "person.js", so that another file

"importPerson.html" can import this file. (see the import default syntax)

// The export file needs to work with the import file.

----

class BassClass { };   // base class

class DerivedClass extends BassClass{ };

// A bass class can be extended by a derived class

// The derived class inherits all properties and methods of the bass class.

e.g.

<script>

class Person {   // bass class

```
name = "Ray Yao";
}
```

class Author extends Person { // derived class extends bass class

```
 show() { return  this.name; }
}
let obj = new Author();
document.write( obj.show() );
</script>
```

// Output: Ray Yao

----

filter() syntax:

array.filter(myFunction)

// Create a new array with array elements that meet the condition.

e.g.

```
<script>
const arr = [1, 2, 3, 4, 5];
document.write(arr.filter(myFun));   // call myFun
function myFun(value, index, array) {
  return value >= 3 ;   // condition
}
</script>
```

// Output: 3, 4, 5

----

find() syntax:

array.find(callback_fucntion);

// "find()" returns the value which is the first element meeting a specified condition.

e.g.

```
<script>
const arr = [10,20,30,40,50,60];
```

```
var first = arr.find(myFun);

document.write( "The first element value greater than 20 is : " + first);

function myFun(value, index) {

  return value > 20;

}
```

</script>

// Output: The first element value greater than 20 is : 30

----

findIndex() syntax:

array.findIndex(callback_fucntion);

// "findIndex()" returns the index which is the first element meeting a specified condition.

e.g.

```
<script>

const arr = [10,20,30,40,50,60];

var first = arr.findIndex(myFun);

document.write( "The first element index whose value is greater than 20 is : " + first);

function myFun(value, index) {

  return value > 20;

}
```

</script>

// Output:

The first element index whose value is greater than 20 is : 2

----

floor() syntax:

Math.floor(argument);

// "Math.floor( );" returns a closest integer that is less than or equal to its argument.

e.g.

```
<script>

var num = 9.5;

document.write ("Flooring number is "+Math.floor( num ));

</script>
```
// Output: Flooring number is 9

----

for…in… syntax:

for (var property in object) {…}

// Iterate over the properties of an object

e.g.

```
<script>

var exam = { Andy: 'A', Betty: 'B', Cindy: 'C' };

for (var mark in exam) {

   document.write(exam[mark] + " ");

}

</script>
```
// Output: A B C

----

for loop syntax:

for(init, test-expression, increment) { // some code; **}**

// "for loop" runs a block of code repeatedly by the specified number of times.

e.g.

```
<script>

for (var x = 0; x <= 5; x++) {     // loop 5 times

document.write ( x );

}

</script>
```
// Output: 012345

----

for (variable of collection){…}

// "for…of…"loops through the values of a string, array, or any collection.

e.g.

```
<script>
// Iterate a string
const str = "HELLO";
var txt = "";
for (var myVar of str) {  txt += myVar + " , ";}
document.write(txt + "<br>");
// Iterate an array
const arr = ["A", "B", "C", "D", "E"];
var val = "";
for (var myVar of arr) {  val += myVar + " , ";}
document.write(val + "<br>");
</script>
// Output:
H , E , L , L , O ,
A , B , C , D , E ,
```

----

foreach() syntax:

array.forEach(myFunction);

// Call a function once for iterating over each array element.

e.g.

```
<script>
const arr = [1, 2, 3, 4, 5];
var str = " ";
arr.forEach(myFun);     // call myFun
document.write(str);
function myFun(value, index, array) {
```

```
  str += value + " ";
}
</script>
// Output:    1,2,3,4,5
```

---

form syntax:

<form name=" " id=" " method=" " action=" ">

</form>

// "form" is used to accept the requests or input data by user.

e.g.

<form name="fm" id="abc" method="get" action="fl.php">

<input name="txt" type="text">

<input name="pwd" type="password">

<input name="rd" type="radio" value="val2">

<input name="chkb" type="checkbox" value="val3">

<input name="sbmt" type="submit" value="Submit">

<input name="rst" type="reset" value="Cancel">

</form>

// Explanation:

// "name" means a name of the form.

// "id" means the id of the form.

// "method="get/post"" means the data send by "get" or "post".

// "get" method sends data openly, small quantity.

// "post" method sends data secretly, more quantity.

// "action=fl.php" means that the data will be processed by fl.php, we can also use fl.asp, or fl.jsp instead.

// "type" specifies the type of element.

// Want to know more? Please see the "Html Css cheat sheet".

---

windows.history.forward();

// "history.forward( )" goes to the next web page.

e.g.

<html>

<button onclick="**history.forward()**">Go Forward</button>

</html>

// Result:

Go forward to the next page when the button is clicked.

----

from syntax:

const obj = Array.from("string");

// "from()" returns an array object form a string.

e.g.

<script>

const arr1 = Array.from("123456789");   // return an array object

document.write(arr1 + " ");

const arr2 = Array.from("JavaScript");   // return an array object

document.write(arr2 + " ");

</script>

// Output: 1,2,3,4,5,6,7,8,9   J,a,v,a,S,c,r,i,p,t

----

fromCharCode() syntax:

String.fromCharCode(unicodes);

// Convert Unicode to a string

e.g.

<script>

var str = **String.fromCharCode(72, 69, 76, 76, 79);**

document.write(str);

</script>

// Output: HELLO

----

function syntax:

function function-name ( ) {......}   // define function

function-name ( );   // call a function

e.g.

```
<html>
<script type="text/JavaScript">
function myFun() {    // define a function
  document.write ("Call a function!");    // output
}
</script>
<body onload = "myFun()">    <!-- call the function -->
</body>
</html>
```

// Output: Call a function!

----

function with argument syntax:

function function-name (var arg) {......}   // define a function

function-name (argument);   // call a function

e.g.

```
<html>
<script type="text/JavaScript">
function test(msg) {   // define a function
  document.write (msg);   // output the value of msg
}
</script>
<body onload=
"test('Call a function with arguments')">
<!-- call the function and pass arguments-->
```

```
</body>
</html>
```

// Output: Call a function with arguments

----

get date, month, year, day, fullyear syntax:

dateObject.getDate( )

dateObject.getMonth( )

dateObject.getYear( )

dateObject.getDay( )

dateObject.getFullYear()

// "getDate()" returns a date.

// "getMonth( )" returns from 0 (January) to 11 (December).

// "getYear( )" returns a year, but need to add 1900.

// "getDay( )" returns from 0 (Sunday) to 6 (Saturday).

// "getFullYear()" returns a year with the correct format.

e.g.

```
<script>
var obj = new Date ( );     // create a date object
var m = obj.getMonth( ) + 1;    // need add 1
var d = obj.getDate( );
var y = obj.getYear( ) + 1900;     // need add 1900
var fy = obj.getFullYear();
var day = obj.getDay();
document.write (  m + " - " + d + " - " + y + "<br>"
+ "This year is  " + fy + "<br>");
document.write ( day );
</script>
```

// Output:

9 - 6 - 2022

This year is 2022

2   // "2" means Tuesday

----

get hours, minutes, seconds syntax:

dateObject.getHours( )   // get the hours

dateObject.getMinutes( )   // get the minutes

dateObject.getSeconds( )   // get the seconds

dateObject.getTime( )   // get the time

// Note that getTime( ) returns a number from January 1,1970 to current time.

e.g.

```
<script>
var now = new Date( );      // create a date object
var h = now.getHours( );
var m = now.getMinutes( );
var s = now.getSeconds( );
document.write ( "The current time is:   ");
document.write ( h + ":" + m + ":" + s );
</script>
// Output:    The current time is: 21:57:40
```

----

get() syntax:

map.get(key)

// Get the value by the specified key in a Map

e.g.

```
<script>
const myMap = new Map([[1, " A"],[2, " B"],[3, " C"]]);
document.write(myMap.get(2));
</script>
```

// Output: B

----

getAttribute() syntax:

getAttribute(attribute);

// "getAttribute(attribute)" returns the value of a specified attribute on an element.

e.g.

```
<html><body>

<p>Hello Dom!</p>

<script>

var text = document.getElementsByTagName("p")[0];

text.setAttribute("align", "center");

// set attribute & value

var value = text.getAttribute( "align" );

// get attribute

document.write( "The 'Hello Dom!' is in the " + value);

</script>

</body></html>
```

// Output: Hello Dom!

The 'Hello Dom!' is in the center

----

getElementById() syntax:

document.getElementById("element").id

// Get the element's id

e.g.

```
<form id="abc" action="">

</form>

<script>

document.write ("The ID of the Form is: "

+ document.getElementById("abc").id);  // get the form's id
```

61

```
</script>
```

// Output: The ID of the Form is: abc

----

getElementById() syntax:

document.getElementById( ).innerHTML = value;

// "getElementById" accesses an element by its id.

// "innerHTML" displays contents in HTML document.

e.g.

```
<html>

<div id = "position"></div>

<script>
```

document.getElementById("position").innerHTML= "OK";

// show "OK" at the specified id "position"

```
</script>

</html>
```

// Output: OK

----

getElementsById().attribute syntax:

document.getElementById(id).attribute = value;

// Assign a value to the element's property

e.g.

```
<html>

<img id="photo" src="img1.gif">


<script>
```

document.getElementById("photo").src="img2.jpg";

```
</script>

</html>
```

// change the img1.gif to img2.jpg

----

getElementById(id).style.property syntax:

62

document.getElementById(id).style.property = value;

//Change the style of the Html element

e.g.

```
<html>

<p id="hi">Hello World!</p>

<script>

document.getElementById("hi").style.color="green";

</script>

</html>
```

// output: Hello World!

----

getElementsByClassName() syntax:

document.getElementsByClassName("MyClass");

// Returns a collection of all elements with the specified class name

e.g.

```
<html>

<div class="MyClass">Element1</div>

<div class="MyClass">Element2</div>

<script>

var collection = document.getElementsByClassName("MyClass");

collection[0].innerHTML = "Very Good!";

</script>

</html>
```

// Output:

Very Good!

Element2

----

getElementsByTagName( ) syntax:

document.getElementsByTagName("tagname").innerHTML

// Get elements by tag name and return a collection. The first element is collection[0], the second is collection[1]……

// "innerHTML" shows or gets the value in HTML document.

e.g.

```
<html>
<ol>
 <li>Red</li>
 <li>Yellow</li>
 <li>Green</li>
</ol>
<button onclick="myFunction()">Click</button>
<p id="S"></p>
<script>
function myFunction() {
var col = document.getElementsByTagName("li");
```

// get all values of all tag "li", such as Red, Yellow, Green, and return a collection "col".

```
document.getElementById("S").innerHTML = col[2].innerHTML;
```

// show the value of col[2] in id "S" when the button is clicked.

```
}
</script>
</html>
```

// Output: Green

----

getter syntax:

get functionName(){ return this.property; }

// Getter method is used to get the property value of the object

e.g.

```
<script>
const speak = {   // create an object
```

64

```
    language: "English",    // object's property and value
    get lang() {   // getter method
      return this.language;
    }
};
document.write(speak.lang);   // Display data using a getter
</script>
// Output:   English
```

----

getTime() syntax:

dateObject.getTime()

// Return the number of milliseconds since January 1, 1970

e.g.

```
<script>
const d = new Date();
document.write(d.getTime());
</script>
// Output:   1663095912096
```

----

getTimezoneOffset( ) syntax:

dateObject. getTimezoneOffset( );

// Return the time difference between UTC time and local time. For example, if your time zone is GMT+2, -120 will be returned.

e.g.

```
<script>
var obj = new Date( );    // create a date object
var diff = obj.getTimezoneOffset( );
document.write ( "The time zone offset is: " + diff );
</script>
// Output:   The time zone offset is: 240
```

----

dateObject.getUTCHours();

// Return the hour of the Greenwich Mean Time.

e.g.

```
<script>
var obj = new Date( );    // create a date object
var utc = obj.getUTCHours( );    // get the hour of utc
document.write ( "The hour of utc is: " + utc )
</script>
// Output:   2
```

----

global variable syntax:

var global_variable = value;   // define a global variable

function function-name (var arg) {......}   // define a function

// A global variable is declared **outside** the function, it can be used in everywhere;

e.g.

```
<html>
<script type="text/JavaScript">
var msg=200;    // This num is a global variable
function myFun(){    // define a function
var msg=100;    // This num is a local variable
}
 document.write (msg);
</script>
<body onload ="myFun()">
</body>
</html>
// Output:   200
```

66

----

window.history.go(number);

// Turn to the specified web page by the number.

e.g.

<html>

<button onclick="**history.history.go(-1)**">Go Back</button>

<button onclick="**history.history.go(1)**">Go Forward</button>

<button onclick="**history.history.go(0)**">Reload</button>

</html>

// Result:

// "<button onclick="history. go(-1)">" goes back to the previous page when the button is clicked.

// "<button onclick="history. go(1)">" goes forward to the next page when the button is clicked.

// "<button onclick="history. go(0)">" reloads the current page when the button is clicked.

----

set.has(value)

// Return true if a Set has the specified value. Otherwise false.

map.has(value)

// Return true if a Map has the specified key. Otherwise false.

e.g.

<script>

const mySet = new Set(["a","b","c"]);

document.write(**mySet.has("a")**);

</script>

// Output: true

e.g.

```
<script>
const myMap = new Map([[1, " A"],[2, " B"],[3, " C"]]);
document.write(myMap.has(2));
</script>
```

// Output: true

----

haschildnodes() syntax:

id.hasChildNodes()

// "hasChildNodes( )" returns true if the specified node has any child nodes, otherwise returns false.

e.g.

```
<html><body>
There are three colors:
<ul id="color">
    <li>Green</li>
    <li>Yellow</li>
    <li>Red</li>
</ul>
<script>
var sub;
sub = document.getElementById("color") .hasChildNodes( );
// check if the "color" id has any child nodes
document.write ("Color has some child nodes?   " + sub );
</script>
</body></html>
```

// Output:

There are three colors:

Green

Yellow

Red

Color has some child nodes? true

----

history.back() syntax:

windows.history.back();

// "history.back( )" goes to the previous web page.

e.g.

\<html\>

\<button onclick="**history.back()**"\>Go Back\</button\>

\</html\>

// Result:

Go back to the previous page when the button is clicked.

----

history.forward() syntax:

windows.history.forward();

// "history.forward( )" goes to the next web page.

e.g.

\<html\>

\<button onclick="**history.forward()**"\>Go Forward\</button\>

\</html\>

// Result:

Go forward to the next page when the button is clicked.

----

history.go() syntax:

window.history.go(number);

// Turn to the specified web page by the number.

e.g.

\<html\>

\<button onclick="**history.history.go(-1)**"\>Go Back\</button\>

\<button onclick="**history.history.go(1)**"\>Go Forward\</button\>

```
<button onclick="history.history.go(0)">Reload</button>
</html>
```

// Result:

// "<button onclick="history. go(-1)">" goes back to the previous page when the button is clicked.

// "<button onclick="history. go(1)">" goes forward to the next page when the button is clicked.

// "<button onclick="history. go(0)">" reloads the current page when the button is clicked.

----

if statement syntax:

if (test-expression) {   // if true do this;   **}**

// "if statement" executes codes inside { … } only if a specified condition is true, does not execute any codes inside {…} if the condition is false.

e.g.

```
<script>
var x=200;
var y=100;
if ( x > y ) {     // if true, do this
document.write ( "x is greater than y" );
}
</script>
```

// Output: x is greater than y

----

if-else statement syntax:

if (test-expression) {   // if true do this;   **}**

else { // if false do this;   **}**

// "if...else statement" runs some code if the condition is true and runs another code if the condition is false

e.g.

```
<script>
```

70

var x=100; var y=200;

if (x>y) {document.write ("x is greater than y.")} // if true do this

else {document.write ("x is less than y");}   // if false do this

</script>

// Output: x is less than y

----

import file syntax:

<script type="module">

import { variable1, variable2 } from "./Export.js";

</script>

// Import data from the export file.

e.g.

<script type="module">

import { name, age } from "./myExport.js";

var txt = "My name is " + name + ". My age is " + age + ".";

document.write(txt);

</script>

// Output: My name is Smith. My age is 17

// Please save this file as "myImport.html" in a folder with the file "myExport.js", so that "myImport.html" can import the data from "myExport.js". (see the export syntax)

// The import file needs to work with the export file by "http://..."

----

import default syntax:

<script type="module">

import function from "./export.js";

<script>

// Import data from the export file.

e.g.

<script type="module">

import person from "./person.js";

document.write(person());

</script>

// Output: Smith is 17 years old.

// Please save this file as "importPerson.html" in a folder with the file "person.js", so that "importPerson.html" can import the data from "person.js". (see the export default syntax)

// The import file needs to work with the export file by "http://..."

----

includes() syntax:

array.includes("value")

// Return true if the array includes the specified value.

e.g.

<script>

const arr = ["Apple", "Banana", "Cherry"];

document.write(**arr.includes("Cherry")**);

</script>

// Output: true

----

includes() syntax:

string.includes(searchvalue, start)

// Return true if a string includes a specified value.

e.g.

<script>

var str = "JavaScript is very easy";

document.write(str.**includes("Java")**);

</script>

// Output: true

----

indexOf() syntax:

array.indexOf(element);

// "indexOf( )" can return the first location where a specified element occurs in an array.

e.g.

```
<script>
var arr = new Array( );
arr[0] ="Mon";
arr[1] ="Tue";
arr[2] ="Wed";
arr[3] ="Tue";
var index = arr.indexOf ("Tue");    // get index of "Tue"
document.write (index);
</script>
// Output:   1
```

----

indexOf() syntax:

string.indexOf(word);

// "indexOf( )" can find the first location where the specified word occurs in a string.

e.g.

```
<script>
var str = "Please do what you decide to do!";
var index = str.indexOf("do");     // return index
document.write ( index );
</script>
// Output:   7
```

----

innerHeight syntax:

var h=window.innerHeight

// Return the internal height of the browser window

e.g.

```
<script>

var h=window.innerHeight

document.write(h);

</script>
```

// Output: 668

----

innerHTML syntax:

document.getElementById( ).innerHTML

// "getElementById" accesses an element by its id.

// "innerHTML" displays contents in HTML document.

e.g.

```
<html>

<div id = "position"></div>

<script>
```

document.getElementById("position").innerHTML= "OK";

// show "OK" at the specified id "position"

```
</script>

</html>
```

// Output: OK

----

innerWidth syntax:

var w=window.innerWidth

// Return the internal height of the browser window

e.g.

```
<script>

var w=window.innerWidth

document.write(w);

</script>
```

```
// Output:   1024
```

---

parent.insertBefore(newElement,child);

// Insert a parent element before the specified child element

e.g.

```
<html>

<div id="myID">

<p id="p1">Text A</p>

<p id="p2">Text B</p>

</div>

<script>     // create a new element

var newElement = document.createElement("p");

var newText = document.createTextNode("New Text");

newElement.appendChild(newText);    // append new text

var parent = document.getElementById("myID");

var child2 = document.getElementById("p2");
```

parent.insertBefore(newElement,child2);   // insert before child2

```
</script>

</html>

// Output:

Text A

New Text

Text B
```

---

var variable = object instanceof type

// Return true if the object is the instance of the object

e.g.

```
<script>
```

```
var fruit = ["Apple", "Banana", "Cherry"];
document.write(fruit instanceof Array);     // return true
document.write(fruit instanceof Object);     // return true
document.write(fruit instanceof Number);     // return false
document.write(fruit instanceof String);     // return false
</script>
```
// Output: true   true   false   false

----

isArray() syntax:

Array.isArray(object)

// Return true if the object is an array

e.g.

```
<script>
const letters = ["A", "B", "C"];
document.write(Array.isArray(letters));
</script>
```
// Output: true

----

isNaN() syntax:

isNaN(value)

// Return true if the value is not a number.

e.g.

```
<script>
var value = 100 / "Hello";     // Nan
document.write(isNaN(value));
</script>
```
// Output: true

----

javaEnabled() syntax:

navigator.javaEnabled( )

// Check if the browser supports Java.

// Note: "navigator" may return an inaccurate information.

e.g.

```
<script>

if ( navigator.javaEnabled( ) == true )

// check if the browser supports Java

document.write ("The browser supports the Java.");

else

document.write ("The browser doesn't support the Java.");

</script>
```

// Output:

The browser supports the Java.

----

join arrays syntax:

array.join( );   // join all array elements without spaces.

array.join(" ");   // join all array elements by spaces.

array.join(" , ");   // join all array elements by commas.

e.g.

```
<script>

var arr = new Array( );

arr[0]="I";

arr[1]="Love";

arr[2]="JavaScript!";

document.write ( arr.join(" ") );     // join by space

</script>
```

// Output: I Love JavaScript!

----

json.parse() syntax:

JSON.parse(string);

// Convert a Json string into a JavaScript object

e.g.

```
<script>

var jsonStr = '{"fruits":[' +

        '{"name":"Apple", "color":"red" },' +

        '{"name":"Banana", "color":"yellow" },' +

        '{"name":"Cherry","color":"purple" }]}';

jsObj = JSON.parse(jsonStr);

// convert 3 json strings to 3 js objects

document.write(jsObj.fruits[0].name + " " + jsObj.fruits[0].color +", ");

document.write(jsObj.fruits[1].name + " " + jsObj.fruits[1].color +", ");

document.write(jsObj.fruits[2].name + " " + jsObj.fruits[2].color +"  ");

</script>

// Output:   Apple red, Banana yellow, Cherry purple
```

----

json.stringify() syntax:

JSON.stringify(object);

// Convert a JavaScript object to a JSON string.

e.g.

```
<script>

var jsObj= {"Firstname":"Andy", "Lastname":"Smith", "Age": "17"}

jsonStr = JSON.stringify(jsObj)

// convert a js object to a json string

document.write("<pre>" + jsonStr + "</pre>" );

</script>

// Output:   {"Firstname":"Andy", "Lastname":"Smith", "Age":"17"}
```

----

key() syntax:

const keys = letters.keys();

// The keys() method returns a new Array iterator object that contains
the keys in the array.

e.g.

```
<script>

const letters = ["A", "B", "C", "D"];

const keys = letters.keys();     // keys is a new Array iterator object

let index = "";

for (let k of keys) {

  index += k + ",";

}

document.write(index);

</script>

// Output:   0,1,2,3,
```

----

lastIndexOf() syntax:

array.lastIndexOf(element);

// "lastIndexOf( )" can return the last location where a specified element occurs in an array.

e.g.

```
<script>

var arr = new Array( );

arr[0] ="Mon"; arr[1] ="Tue"; arr[2] ="Wed"; arr[3] ="Tue";

var index=arr.lastIndexOf ( "Tue" );    // get index of "Tue"

document.write (index);

</script>

// Output:   3
```

----

lastIndexOf() syntax:

array.lastIndexOf(word);

// "lastIndexOf( )" can return the last location where a specified word occurs in a string.

e.g.

```
<script>
var str = "Please do what you decide to do!";
var index = str.lastIndexOf("do");    // return index
document.write( index );
</script>
// Output:   29
```

----

let syntax:

let variable;   // declare a variable

let variable = value;   // define a variable with a value

e.g.

```
<script>
let x, y, z;     // declare three variables
let str = "Hello ";     // define a variable "str" with a value
x = 100; y = 200;
z = x + y;
document.write(str);
document.write(z);
</script>
// Output:   Hello  300
```

----

link() syntax:

string.link(String)

// "string.link(String)" adds a hyperlink to a string.

e.g.

```
<script>
var str = "Please click me!";
var L = str.link("https://www.amazon.com/author/ray-yao");
// add a hyperlink to the string
```

```
document.write ("Welcome to our website:  " + L);
</script>
// Output:   Welcome to our website: Please click me!
```

----

local variable syntax:

function function-name (var arg) {   // define a function

var local_variable = value;   // define a local variable

}

// A local variable is declared **inside** a function, it can be used in the current function only;

e.g.

```
<html>
<script type="text/JavaScript">
var msg=200;    // This num is a global variable
function myFun(){      // define a function
var msg=100;       // This num is a local variable
document.write (msg);
}
</script>
<body onload ="myFun()">
</body>
</html>
// Output:   100
```

----

location.assign() syntax:

window.location.assign("url");

// Assign a new page to current page by the specified url.

e.g.

```
<html>
<script>
```

```
function newPage(){
```

window.location.assign("https://www.amazon.com")

```
}
```

```
</script>
```

```
<input type="button" value="Load New Page" onclick="newPage()">
```

```
</html>
```

// Output: (We can see the web page of Amazon)

----

location.href syntax:

document.write(location.href);

// Show the url of the current page

e.g.

```
<script>
```

```
document.write(location.href);
```

```
</script>
```

// Output: www.amazon.com/author/ray-yao

----

location.pathname syntax:

location.pathname   // get the file pathname of url

e.g.

```
<script>
```

document.write(**location.pathname**);

```
</script>
```

// Output: /C:/Users/RAY/Documents/w001.html

----

map() syntax:

array.map(myFunction)

// Create a new array by running a function on each array element

```
<script>
```

```
const arr = [1, 2, 3, 4, 5];
```

82

```
document.write(arr.map(myFun));   // call myFun
function myFun(value, index, array) {
  return value + 10 ;
}
</script>
// Output:   11,12,13,14,15
```

----

match() syntax:

string.search(regexp);

// Execute a search for a match between a regular expression and a
specified string. Return the matched characters if successful, otherwise
return null.

e.g.

```
<script>
var text = "JavaScript is very easy";
document.write(text.match(/Java/g));
</script>
// Output:   Java
```

Math Constant syntax:

Math.Property

// There are 8 JavaScript Math constants which can be accessed as
Math properties

e.g.

```
<script>
document.write(
"<p>Math.E: " + Math.E + "</p>" +
"<p>Math.PI: " + Math.PI + "</p>" +
"<p>Math.SQRT2: " + Math.SQRT2 + "</p>" +
"<p>Math.SQRT1_2: " + Math.SQRT1_2 + "</p>" +
```

```
"<p>Math.LN2: " + Math.LN2 + "</p>" +

"<p>Math.LN10: " + Math.LN10 + "</p>" +

"<p>Math.LOG2E: " + Math.LOG2E + "</p>" +

"<p>Math.Log10E: " + Math.LOG10E + "</p>");
</script>
```

// Output:

Math.E: 2.718281828459045

Math.PI: 3.141592653589793

Math.SQRT2: 1.4142135623730951

Math.SQRT1_2: 0.7071067811865476

Math.LN2: 0.6931471805599453

Math.LN10: 2.302585092994046

Math.LOG2E: 1.4426950408889634

Math.Log10E: 0.4342944819032518

Math.max.apply() syntax:

Math.max.apply(this, array);

// Return the maximum value of the array element

e.g.

```
<script>
const myArr = [10,20,30,40,50,60];

document.write(Math.max.apply(this, myArr));
</script>
```

// Output: 60

Math.min.apply() syntax:

Math.min.apply(this, array);

// Return the minimum value of the array element

e.g.

```
<script>
```

```
const myArr = [10,20,30,40,50,60];

document.write(Math.min.apply(this, myArr));

</script>
```

// Output: 10

Math.max(num1, num2);

// Return the greater one between two numbers.

e.g.

```
<script>

var x = 100;

var y = 200;

document.write ("Greater number is "+Math.max(x, y));

</script>
```

// Output: Greater number is 200

NUMBER.MAX_VALUE

// MAX_VALUE returns the largest number in JavaScript

e.g.

```
<script>

document.write(Number.MAX_VALUE);

</script>
```

// Output: 1.7976931348623157e+308

Math.min(num1, num2);

// Return the less one between two numbers.

e.g.

```
<script>
```

```
var x = 100;
var y = 200;
document.write ("Less number is "+Math.min(x, y));
</script>
```

// Output: Less number is 100

MIN_VALUE syntax:

NUMBER.MIN_VALUE

// MIN_VALUE returns the smallest number in JavaScript

e.g.

```
<script>

document.write(Number.MIN_VALUE);

</script>
```

// Output: 5e-324

NaN syntax:

NaN

// NaN indicates that it is not a number.

e.g.

```
<script>
document.write(100 / "hello");
</script>
```

// Output: NaN

----

navigator syntax:

navigator.appCodeName   // get the browser code

navigator.appName   // get the browser name

navigator.appVersion   // get the browser version

navigator.platform   // get the browser platform

navigator.userAgent   // get the browser agent

navigator.language   // get the browser language

navigator.cookieEnabled   // return true if cookie is enabled

navigator.javaEnabled()   // return true if Java is enabled

// Note: "navigator" may return an inaccurate information.

e.g.

```
<script>
info = "<p>Browser Code: " + navigator.appCodeName + "</p>";
info+= "<p>Browser Name: " + navigator.appName + "</p>";
info+= "<p>Browser Version: " + navigator.appVersion + "</p>";
info+= "<p>Browser Platform: " + navigator.platform + "</p>";
info+= "<p>Browser Agent: " + navigator.userAgent + "</p>";
info+= "<p>Browser Language: " + navigator.language + "</p>";
info+= "<p>Cookies Enabled: " + navigator.cookieEnabled + "</p>";
info+= "<p>Java Enabled: " + navigator.javaEnabled() + "</p>";
document.write(info);
</script>
// Output:
Browser Code: Mozilla
Browser Name: Netscape
Browser Version: 5.0 (Windows NT 6.3; WOW64) AppleWebKit/537.36
(KHTML, like Gecko) Chrome/86.0.4240.198 Safari/537.36
Browser Platform: Win32
Browser Agent: Mozilla/5.0 (Windows NT 6.3; WOW64)
AppleWebKit/537.36 (KHTML, like Gecko) Chrome/86.0.4240.198
Safari/537.36
Browser Language: en-US
Cookies Enabled: true
Java Enabled: false
```

NEGATIVE_INFINITY syntax:

Number.NEGATIVE_INFINITY;

// NEGATIVE_INFINITY means negative infinity, returns overflow

e.g.

```
<script>

let num = Number.NEGATIVE_INFINITY;

document.write(num);

</script>

// Output:   -Infinity
```

----

nodeValue syntax:

document.getElementById("").childNodes[index].nodeValue);

// Get the node value of the specified node

// "parentNode, firstNode, lastNode" can also access node.

e.g.

```
<html>

<p id="id00">A</p><p id="id01">B</p><p id="id02">C</p>

<script>

document.write( "The node value of the id01 is: " +

document.getElementById("id01").childNodes[0].nodeValue);

</script>

</html>

// Output:   A  B  C     The node value of the id01 is: B
```

----

now() syntax:

const milliseconds = Date.now();

// Return the number of milliseconds elapsed since January 1, 1970.

e.g.

```
<script>

const milliseconds = Date.now();

document.write(milliseconds);
```

```
</script>
```
// Output: 1663717971688

----

null syntax:

var variable = null;

// "null" is a special value that means an empty or unknown value.

// The type of the null is "object". Note: "null" is not "undefined".

e.g.

```
<script>
```
let number = null;

document.write(typeof number);

```
</script>
```
// Output: object

----

number() syntax:

Number(parameter)

// Number(parameter) converts its parameter to a number.

e.g.

```
<script>
```
document.write(**Number(true)+" "+Number("100")**);

```
</script>
```
// Output: 1   100

----

object creating syntax:

obj = new Object( );   // create an object

obj.property;   // object's property

obj.method();   // object's method

e.g.

```
<script>
```
house = new Object( );   // create an object "house"

```
var size = "large";

var price = "expensive";

function build(){ return "good!" };

document.write ( "House size:  " + this.size + "<br>" );

document.write ( "House price:  " + this.price + "<br>");

document.write ( "House building:  " + this.build() + "<br>" );

</script>
```

// Output:

House size: large

House price: expensive

House building: good!

----

object creating syntax:

const object = { property1:value1, property2: value2,

property: function(){}, …}

// One object can contain multiple properties and functions.

e.g.

```
<script>
```

const house = { size:"large", price:"expensive",

build:function(){return "good!"} };   // create an object "house"

```
document.write("The size of the house is " + house.size + "<br>");

document.write("The price of the house is " + house.price + "<br>");

document.write("The building of the house is " + house.build() + "<br>");

</script>
```

// Output:

The size of the house is large

The price of the house is expensive

The building of the house is good!

----

onblur syntax:

onBlur = "function( )"

// onBlur = "function( )" means when a user moves the cursor out of an element and clicks other area on the web page, the function will run at once, a blur event occurs.

e.g.

<html>

<script>

function myfunction( )

{ confirm ("Are you sure to leave?");}

</script>   <!-- blur event -->

<input type="text" **onBlur="myfunction( )"**>

</html>

// Output: Are you sure to leave?

----

onchange syntax:

onChange = "function()"

// onChange = "function( );" means when the contents of an element is changed, the function immediately runs. The change event occurs.

e.g.

<html>

<script language="javascript">

function myfun(color){

alert ("The flower is "+ color);

}   // assume that we select "Red" option

</script>

<form id="myForm">

<select name="flower" onChange="myfun(this.value)">

<option value="Green">Green</option>

<option value="Yellow">Yellow</option>

<option value="Red">Red</option>

</select>

```
</html>
```

// Output: The flower is Red

----

onclick syntax:

onClick = "function( )"

// onClick = "function( );" means when an element is clicked, a function immediately runs. The click event occurs.

e.g.

```
<form>
<input type="button" value="Previous" onClick="history.back( )">
</form>
```

// Result:

// "onClick="history.back( )"" means when the button is clicked, the "history.back( )" runs at once, and then go back to the previous web page.

----

onfocus syntax:

onFocus = "function( )"

// onFocus = "function( )" means when a user moves the cursor onto an element of the web page, a function( ) immediately executes.

e.g.

```
<html>
<script>
function myfunction( )
{ confirm ("Are you ready to input data?"); }
</script>
<!-- focus event -->
<input type="text" onFocus ="myfunction( )">
</html>
```

// Output: Are you ready to input data?

----

onKeyDown = "function()"

// onKeyDown = "function( )" executes the function when a key is down.

e.g.

```
<html><script type="text/JavaScript">
function myFunction(msg) {
  alert(msg);
}
</script>
<body onKeyDown="myFunction('Hello! My Friend.')">
Please press down a key.
</body></html>
```

// Output: Hello! My Friend.

----

onkeypress syntax:

onKeyPress = "function( )"

// onKeyPress = "function( )" executes the function when a key is pressed.

e.g.

```
<html><script type="text/JavaScript">
function myFunction(msg) {
  alert(msg);
}
</script>
<body onKeyPress="myFunction('Hello! My Friend.')">
Please press a key.
</body></html>
```

// Output: Hello! My Friend.

----

onkeyup syntax:

onKeyUp = "function( )"

// onKeyUp = "function( )" means when a key is released, a function( ) runs immediately.

e.g.

```
<html><script type="text/JavaScript">

function myFunction(msg) { document.write (msg);}

</script>

<body onKeyUp ="myFunction('KeyUp event occurs!')">

Please press a key, and release.

</body></html>
```

// Output: KeyUp event occurs!

----

onload syntax:

onLoad = "function( )"

// onLoad = "function( )" executes the function when a web page has been loaded.

e.g.

```
<html><body onLoad = "myFun()">   <!-- load event -->

<script>

function myFun(){

document.write ("Welcome to my website!");

}

</script>

</body></html>
```

// Output: Welcome to my website!

----

onmouseout syntax:

onMouseOut = "function( )"

// onMouseOut = "function( )" means when the mouse pointer moves out of an element, function( ) runs immediately.

94

e.g.

```
<html><script type="text/javascript">
function myfunction() { alert ("See You!"); }
</script>
<body>
<textarea onMouseOut ="myfunction()">
 move the mouse away.</textarea>
</body></html>
// Output:   See You!
```

----

onmouseover syntax:

onMouseOver = "function( )"

// onMouseOver = "function( )" executes the function immediately when the mouse moves over an element.

e.g.

```
<html><script type="text/JavaScript">
function myFunction() {
 alert ("MouseOver event occurs!");
}
</script>
<body>     <!-- mouseover event -->
<textarea onMouseOver ="myFunction()">
Put the mouse on me!</textarea>
</body></html>
// Output:   MouseOver event occurs!
```

----

onreset syntax:

onReset = "function( )"

// onReset = "function( )" executes the "function( )" when the form is reset.

e.g.

```html
<html>
<form onReset = "alert('The form has been reset!')">
<input type = "text" id = "txt">
<input type = "reset" value = "Reset" >
<!-- reset event -->
</form>
</html>
// Output:   The form has been reset!
```

----

onsubmit syntax:

onSubmit = "function( )"

// onSubmit = "function( )" executes the "function( )" when the form is submitted.

e.g.

```html
<html>
<form onSubmit = "alert('The form has been submitted!')">
<input type = "text" id = "txt">
<input type = "submit" value = "Submit" >
<!-- submit event -->
</form>
</html>
// Output:   The form has been submitted!
```

----

open() syntax:

window.open(url, name, width, height, status, menubar, toolbar)

// "window.open" can open a new customized window.

// "url" argument means new window url.

// "name" argument means new window name.

// "width" argument means the new window's width.

// "height" argument means the new window's height.

// "status" argument defines window's status bar.

// "menubar" argument defines window's menu bar.

// "toolbar" argument defines the window's toolbar.

e.g.

```
<html>

<script>

function openWindow(){

windowObj = window.open(" ","MyWindow",    "height=200, width=350,

toolbar=yes, menubar=yes, status=no, top=200, left=200");   // open a

customized window & create an object

windowObj.document.write ("This is a new window.");

}

</script>

<form><center><input type="button" onClick="openWindow()"

value="Open Window"></center></form>

</html>
```

// Result: Open a new window when the button is clicked

----

padEnd() syntax:

string.padEnd(length, character);

// Pad the end side of the string by specified characters and length

e.g.

```
<script>

var str = "Hi";

document.write(str.padEnd(5,"0"));

</script>
```

// Output: Hi000

----

string.padStart(length, character);

// Pad the start side of the string by specified characters and length

e.g.

<script>

var str = "Hi";

document.write(str.**padStart(5,"0")**);

</script>

// Output: 000Hi

Date.parse(dateObject);

// Return the number of milliseconds between January 1, 1970 and specified date.

e.g.

<script>

var d = new Date (2010, 10, 1);   // create a date object

var result = **Date.parse(d)**;

// get the milliseconds from January 1, 1970 to specified date

document.write (result);

</script>

// Output: 1288587600000

----

parseFloat(string);

// "parseFloat(string)" can convert a string to a floating point number.

e.g.

<script>

```
var str1 = "12.66";  var str2 = "68.22";
var num1 = parseFloat( str1 );       // convert to Float
var num2 = parseFloat( str2 );       // convert to Float
var addition = num1 + num2;     // add instead of join
document.write ( addition );
</script>
// Output:   80.88
```

----

parseInt() syntax:

parseInt(string);

// "parseInt(string)" can convert a string to an integer number.

e.g.

```
<script>
var str1 = "12";  var str2 = "68";
var num1 = parseInt( str1 );      // convert to integer
var num2 = parseInt( str2 );      // convert to integer
var addition = num1 + num2;     // add instead of join
document.write ( addition );
</script>
// Output:   80
```

----

pi syntax:

Math.PI;

// Math.PI is a constant that stores the value of pi.

e.g.

```
<script>
var pi = Math.PI;
document.write ("The PI value is " + pi);
</script>
// Output:   The PI value is 3.141592653589793
```

----

array.pop();

// Remove the last element of an array.

e.g.

```
<script>

var arr = [1,2,3,4,5,6];

arr.pop( );     // remove the last element of arr

document.write (arr);

</script>
```

// Output: 1,2,3,4,5

POSITIVE_INFINITY syntax:

Number.POSITIVE_INFINITY;

// POSITIVE_INFINITY means infinity, returns overflow

e.g.

```
<script>

let num = Number.POSITIVE_INFINITY;

document.write(num);

</script>
```

// Output: Infinity

----

pow() syntax:

Math.pow(x, y);

// Return the value of x to the power of y. Namely (x^y)

e.g.

```
<script>

var result = Math.pow(6, 2);

document.write ( result );

</script>
```

// Output: 36

----

print() syntax:

window.print( )

// print the contents of the current window.

e.g.

<script>

function printWin( ){

window.print( );   // print the current window

}

</script>

<form>

<input type="button" onclick="printWin( )" value="Print">

</form>

// Click "Print" button to print the content of the current page

----

promise() syntax:

new Promise(function(resolve, reject) {…}

// Promise() can complete asynchronous tasks

// "resolve" is used when the program running is normal.

// "reject" is used when an exception occurs.

e.g.

<script>

new Promise(function(resolve, reject) {

var a = 100; var b = 1;

if (b == 0) **reject**("Divide zero, exception occurs!");

else **resolve**(document.write(a / b));

})

</script>

// Output: 100

----

window.prompt( );

// Prompt user to input something in a dialog box, for example, an user enters "Yes, I like it.", and then click the "OK" or "Cancel" button.

e.g.

<script>

var data = **window.prompt** ("Do you like JavaScript?");

// prompt user to input something in dialog box.

 // prompt() stores the inputted contents to the "data"

document.write(data);

</script>

// Output: The message you have just inputted.

----

prototype syntax:

Object.prototype.variable = value;

// Prototype can provide additional property to the object created by a constructor function.

e.g.

<script>

function Person(name, age) {   // constructor

  this.name = name;

  this.age = age;

}

Person.prototype.gender = "Female";   // add a property

const student = new Person("Rosy", 16);   // Create an object

document.write("The student is " + student.name +"<br>");

document.write("The student is " + student.age +"<br>");

document.write("The student is " + student.gender +"<br>");

</script>

// Output:

The student is Rosy

The student is 16

The student is Female

----

push() syntax:

array.push();

// Add one or more elements to the end of an array.

e.g.

```
<script>
var arr = [1,2,3];
arr.push( 4, 5, 6 );      // add 4,5,6 to the end of "arr"
document.write (arr);
</script>
```

// Output: 1,2,3,4,5,6

----

querySelectorAll() syntax:

var nodeList = document.querySelectorAll("tagName");

// Query all elements by tag name, and return a nodeList collection. The first list is list[0], the second list is list[1]……

nodeList.length   // get the length of the nodeList collection.

e.g.

```
<html>
<p>Text A</p>
<p>Text B</p>
<script>
var list = document.querySelectorAll("p");
document.write("There are " + list.length + " lists<br>");
document.write ("The second P contains " + list[1].innerHTML );
</script>
```

```
</html>
// Output:
Text A
Text B
There are 2 lists
The second P contains Text B
```

----

radio syntax:

`<input type="radio" name= "same" value= "myValue">`

```
// A group of radio buttons allows one circle to be checked at any time
and submit the selected value to handle.
// Note: each radio name must be the same.
e.g.
<html><body>
<form name="myform">
<input type= "radio"  name="color" value= "Red" onClick=
"myfun(this.value )"/> Red
<input type= "radio"  name="color" value= "Yellow" onClick=
"myfun(this.value )"/> Yellow
<input type= "radio"  name="color" value= "Green" onClick=
"myfun(this.value )"/> Green
</form>
<script>
function myfun( v) {
alert ( "You select:  " + v );
}    // assume that we click Green radio button
</script>
</body></html>
// Output:   You select:  Green
```

----

random() syntax:

Math.random();

// Math.random( ) generates a number between 0.0 to 1.0.

e.g.

\<script\>

var ran = **Math.random( )**;

document.write ("The random number is " + ran);

\</script\>

// Output: The random number is 0.2888501447159797

----

reduce() syntax:

array.reduce(function(lastValue, nowValue) {

return lastValue operator nowValue;

});

// "reduce()" can reduce an array to a value.

// "reduce()" uses a single operator to continuously evaluate each array element value.

e.g.

\<script\>

var arr = [10, 20, 30, 40]; // firstly, "10" is lastValue, "20" is nowValue

var sum = **arr.reduce(function(lastValue, nowValue) {**

return lastValue + nowValue;   // using "+" operator

});   // 10 + 20 + 30 + 40 = 100

document.write(sum);

\</script\>

// Output: 100

e.g.

\<script\>

var arr = [10, 20, 30, 40]; // firstly, "10" is lastValue, "20" is nowValue

var difference = **arr.reduce(function(lastValue, nowValue) {**

105

return lastValue - nowValue;   // using "-" operator

});   // 10 - 20 - 30 - 40 = -80

document.write(difference);

</script>

// Output: -80

RegExp() syntax:

var pattern = new RegExp(/characters/modifier);

// A regular expression is a search pattern formed by a sequence of characters

// "modifier" means case incentive "i", global "g", multi-lines "m".

e.g.

<script>

var patt=new RegExp(/Visual Basic/i);   // regular expression

document.write(patt.test("visual basic"));

</script>

// Output: true

----

regular expression syntax:

/ characters / modifier

// A regular expression is a search pattern formed by a sequence of characters

// "modifier" means case incentive "i", global "g", multi-lines "m".

e.g.

<script>

var str = "Visual Basic";

var index = **str.search(/basic/i);**

document.write(index);

</script>

// Output: 7

----

remove() syntax:

document.getElementById("myId").remove();

// Remove the specified element according to the id

e.g.

<html>

<div>

<p id="id01">Text A</p>

<p id="id02">Text B</p>

</div>

<script>

document.getElementById("id01").remove();

</script>

</html>

// Output: Text B

----

removeChild() syntax:

parent.removeChild(child);

// Remove a child element with the parent element

e.g.

<html>

<div id="myID">

<p id="id1">Text A</p>

<p id="id2">Text B</p>

</div>

<script>

var parent = document.getElementById("myID");

var child1 = document.getElementById("id1");

parent.removeChild(child1);   // remove Text A

</script>

```
</html>
```

// Output: Text B

----

removeEventListener() syntax:

element.removeEventListener("event", function);

// Remove the event listener added by addEventListener() method

e.g.

```
<html>
<h1 id="hover">1. Hover Over Here First!</h1>
<button onclick="clicking()">2. Click Me!</button><br>
<b id="result"></b>
<script>
const text = document.getElementById("hover");
text.addEventListener("mouseover", hoverFun);
function hoverFun() {
document.getElementById("result").innerHTML += "<br>"+"mouseover
Event occurs!" + "<br>";}
function clicking() {
```

text.removeEventListener("mouseover", hoverFun);

```
document.getElementById("result").innerHTML += "<br>"+
'Because you clicked the "Click Me!" button,' + "<br>" +"now the
mouseover event listener has been removed!";}
</script>
</html>
```

// Output:

1. Hover Over Here First!

    2. Click Me!

mouseover Event occurs!

mouseover Event occurs!

Because you clicked the "Click Me!" button,

now the mouseover event listener has been removed!

<div align="center">**replace() syntax:**</div>

str.replace("string1", "string2");

// Replace the string1 value with string2 value

// The replace() method is case sensitive by default

// To replace case insensitive, use (/string1/i, "string2")

e.g.

<script>

var str = "JavaScript is easy.";

var text = **str.replace("JavaScript", "Python");**

document.write (text);

</script>

// Output: Python is easy

<div align="center">**replaceChild() syntax:**</div>

parent.replaceChild(newElement,child);

// Replace a specified child element with the parent element

e.g.

<html>

<div id="myID">

<p id="p1">Text A</p>

<p id="p2">Text B</p>

</div>

<script>   // create a new element

var newElement = document.createElement("p");

var newText = document.createTextNode("New Text");

newElement.appendChild(newText);   // append new text

var parent = document.getElementById("myID");

var child2 = document.getElementById("p2");

parent.replaceChild(newElement,child2);   // replace child2

```
</script>

</html>

// Output:

Text A

New Text
```

----

required="required"

// Required attribute will prevent the form from being submitted If the value of the form field is empty.

e.g.

```
<form action="myfile.php" method="post">

<input type="text" name="name" required="required">

<input type="submit" value="Submit">

</form>
```

// The text field is required to be inputted some contents

----

form.reset

// "reset( )" is used to clear the form data.

e.g.

```
<html>

<form id="myform" >

<textarea></textarea>

<br><br>

<input type="button" onClick="fun()" value="Clear" >

</form>

<script type="text/javascript">

function fun() {

document.getElementById("myform").reset();
```

}   // "reset( )" clears "myform" data in textarea

</script>

</html>

// Result:

// When the "clear" button is clicked, the form data are completely cleared.

----

return syntax:

function function-name (var arg) { return value }

// define a function, return the value to the function caller

function-name (argument);

 // call the function

e.g.

<script language="javascript">

function add(num1,num2){   // define a function

return num1+num2;   // pass the result to the function caller

}

document.write ("3 + 5 = " + **add(3, 5)**);   // function caller

</script>

// Output: 3 + 5 = 8

----

reverse array syntax:

array.reverse( );

// Reverse the element order of an array.

e.g.

<script>

var arr = new Array("A", "B", "C");

arr.reverse( );   // reverse the element order

var rev = arr.join(",");   // join all elements by ","

document.write (rev);

111

```
</script>
```
// Output: C,B,A

---

round() syntax:

Math.round();

// Return an integer

e.g.

```
<script>
var num = 10.5;
document.write ( Math.round(num) );
</script>
```
// Output: 11

---

screen.height syntax:

screen.height

// return the height of the screen.

e.g.

```
<script>
var h = screen.height;
document.write ( h );
</script>
```
// Output: 768

---

screen.width syntax:

screen.width

// return the width of the screen.

e.g.

```
<script>
var w = screen.width;
document.write ( w );
```

```
</script>
```
// Output: 1024

----

search() syntax:

string.search("value")

// Search a string for a specified value and return an index

e.g.

```
<script>
var str = "JavaScript is very easy";
document.write(str.search("is"));
</script>
```

// Output: 11

----

select menu syntax:

<select id="myID " onchange="function ( )">

<option value="AAA">AAA</option>

<option value="BBB">BBB</option>

<option value="CCC">CCC</option>

</select>

// When a "select" value in the form is changed, "onChange" event
occurs and runs the "function ( )" at once.

e.g.

```
<html>
<script language="javascript">
function myfun(color){
alert ("The flower is  "+ color);
}     // assume that we select "Red" option
</script>
<form id="myForm">
```
<select name="flower" onChange="myfun(this.value)">

```
<option value="Green">Green</option>

<option value="Yellow">Yellow</option>

<option value="Red">Red</option>

</select>

</html>

// Output:   The flower is Red
```

----

self-invoked function syntax:

(function () {.....})();

// "()" can call the self-invoked function.

e.g.

```
<script>

( function () {

    document.write( "I am a self-invoked function" );

})();   // "()" can call the self-invoked function

</script>

// Output:   I am a self-invoked function
```

----

set date, month, year syntax:

dateObject.setDate();   // set a date

dateObject.setMonth();   // set a month

dateObject.setFullYear();   // set a year

e.g.

```
<script>

var obj = new Date();      // create a date object

obj.setDate(18);

obj.setMonth(0);

obj.setFullYear(2016);

var today = obj;

document.write (today);
```

```
</script>
```

// Output:

Mon Jan 18 2016 08:54:16 GMT-0500 (Eastern Time)

----

set hours, minutes, seconds syntax:

dateObject.setHours( );   // set the hours

dateObject.setMinutes( );   // set the minutes

dateObject.setSeconds( );   // set the seconds

e.g.

```
<script>
var obj = new Date();    // create a date object
obj.setHours(9);
obj.setMinutes(30);
obj.setSeconds(18);
var now = obj;
document.write (now);
</script>
```

// Output:

Wed Sep 07 2022 09:30:18 GMT-0400 (Eastern Time)

Set creating syntax:

const mySet = new Set([val1, val2, val3,…]);

// Set is a collection that only has unique values.

e.g.

```
<script>
const mySet = new Set(["A","B","C"]);    // Create a Set
document.write(mySet.size);    // show the size of mySet
</script>
```

// Output: 3

----

map.set(key, value);

// Set a key/value pair in a Map.

e.g

```
<script>
const myMap = new Map();
  myMap.set(1, " A");
  myMap.set(2, " B");
  myMap.set(3, " C");
document.write(myMap.get(2));
</script>
// Output:   B
```

----

setAttribute() syntax:

setAttribute(attribute, value);

// "setAttribute(attribute, value)" adds the specified attribute and specified value to an element.

e.g.

```
<html><body>
<p>Hello Dom!</p>
<script>
var text = document.getElementsByTagName("p")[0];
text.setAttribute("align", "center");
// set attribute & value
var value = text.getAttribute( "align" );
// get attribute
document.write( "The 'Hello Dom!' is in the " + value);
</script>
</body></html>
// Output:    Hello Dom!
```

The 'Hello Dom!' is in the center

----

setCustomValidity() syntax:

input.setCustomValidity("message");

// Set validity message

e.g.

<html>

<input id="fm" type="number" min="100" max="300" required>

<button onclick="myFun()">Check</button>

<script>

function myFun() {

var num = document.getElementById("fm");

if (num.checkValidity() == false) {

if(num.value==""){

num.setCustomValidity("Cannot be empty!");

}else if(num.value<100 || num.value>300){

num.setCustomValidity("Please input a number between 100 and 300!");}

document.write(num.validationMessage);

} else {

document.write("Correct Input");

}}

</script>

</html>

// Output: Cannot be empty!

        Please input a number between 100 and 300!"

----

setInterval() syntax:

setInterval(function(){},milliseconds);

// Execute the specified code continuously according to the milliseconds of the interval

e.g.

```html
<html>
<button onclick="myFun()">Click Me</button>
<script>
function myFun(){
setInterval(function(){alert("Hello")},3000);
}
</script>
</html>
// Output:   Hello
```

----

setter syntax:

```
set method(arg){   // setter method
this.property = arg;
}};
object.method = value;   // set value
```

// Setter method is used to set the property values of the object.

e.g.

```html
<script>
const student = {     // create an object
name: "No",     // object's property and value
set change(newName){   // setter method
this.name = newName;
}};
student.change = "Nancy";   // set object property value
document.write(student.name);
</script>
// Output:   Nancy
```

----

dateObject.setTime(milliseconds);

// Set date and time by adding the milliseconds since 1/1/1970.

e.g.

<script>

const d = new Date();

d.setTime(1656533882698);

document.write(d);

</script>

// Output: Wed Jun 29 2022 16:18:02 GMT-0400 (Eastern Time)

----

window.setTimeout("function()", milliseconds);

// "window.setTimeout()" can set the interval time to call the function() repeatedly.

e.g.

<html>

<body onload="autoTimer()">

<script>

var count=0;

function autoTimer( ) {   // user-defined function

count++;

if (count <= 9) {

document.write (count);   // show the increasing numbers

window.setTimeout("autoTimer()" , 1000);

// call autoTime() every other 1 seconds

}}

</script>

</body>

```
</html>
```

// Output: 123456789

---

shift() syntax:

array.shift();

// Remove the first element of an array.

e.g.

```
<script>
var arr = [4,5,6];
arr.shift( );     // remove the first element of the array
document.write (arr);
</script>
```

// Output: 5,6

---

sign() syntax:

Math.sign(number)

// Return 1 if the number is positive, return 0 if the number is zero, return -1 if the number is negative.

e.g.

```
<script>
document.write(Math.sign(10) + " ");
document.write(Math.sign(0) + " ");
document.write(Math.sign(-10) + " ");
</script>
```

// Output: 1   0   -1

---

sin() syntax:

Math.sin(radian)

// Return the sine value of a radian.

e.g.

```
<script>

document.write(Math.sin(3.14).toFixed(2));

</script>
```

// Output: 0.00

----

size syntax:

set.size   or   **map.size**

// Get the size of a Set or a Map

e.g.

```
<script>

const mySet = new Set(["a","b","c"]);

document.write(" mySet size " + mySet.size + " , ");

const myMap = new Map([[1, " A"],[2, " B"],[3, " C"]]);

document.write(" myMap size " + myMap.size + " ");

</script>
```

// Output: mySet size 3 ,   myMap size 3

----

slice array syntax:

array.slice(start, last-1);

// "array.slice(start, last-1)" can slice array elements into pieces,

extracts some elements from start to last-1 index. Index starts from 0

// "start" means the first element.

// "last-1" means the last-1 element.

e.g.

```
<script>

var arr = new Array(  "a", "b", "c", "d", "e", "f" );

var sli = arr.slice( 2, 5 );
```

// extract some elements from index 2 to index 5-1

```
document.write ( sli );

</script>
```

// Output: c, d, e

----

slice string syntax:

string.slice(start, last-1);

// "string.slice(start, last-1)" can slice string letters into pieces, extracts some letters from start to last-1 index. Index starts from 0.

// "start" means the first letter.

// "last-1" means the last-1 letter.

e.g.

<script>

var str = "PowerShell";

var s = **str.slice(5, 8);**

// extract some letters from index 5 to index 8-1

document.write (s);

</script>

// Output: She

----

slice array syntax:

newArray = array.slice(index);

// Slice a portion of an array and become a new array

// "index" specifies that the position to start slicing

e.g.

<script>

const arr = ["A", "B", "C", "D", "E"];

const newArr = **arr.slice(2);**

document.write(newArr);

</script>

// Output: "C", "D", "E"

----

some() syntax:

array.some(callback_fucntion);

// "some()" checks if some element values meet a specified condition.

// Return true if some element values meet a specified condition.

e.g.

```
<script>
const arr = [10,20,30,40,50,60];
var num = arr.some(myFun);
document.write("Are some element values greater than 20 ?  " + num);
function myFun(value) {
  return value > 20;  // check if some element values are greater than 20
}
</script>
```

// Output: Are some element values greater than 20 ? true

----

sort array syntax:

array.sort( );

// "array.sort( )" can sort array elements orderly.

e.g.

```
<script>
var arr = new Array( 2, 5, 3, 1, 4, 6 );
arr.sort ( );     // sort all elements in order
var s = arr.join(",");     // join all elements by ","
document.write ( s );
</script>
```

// Output: 1,2,3,4,5,6

----

split() syntax:

string.split(",")   // Split on commas

string.split(" ")   // Split on spaces

string.split("|")   // Split on pipe

// "split(" ")" can split a string into multiple substrings by the spaces in the string. But the separators are commas ",".

// "split()" is also used to convert a string into an array.

e.g.

```
<script>
var str = "JavaScript for Beginners";
var substr = str.split( " " );  /* split str into substrings according to the spaces of str */
document.write ( substr );    // shows substrings
document.write ( "<br>" + substr[0]);
document.write ( "<br>" + substr[1]);
document.write ( "<br>" + substr[2]);
</script>
// Output:
JavaScript , for , Beginners
JavaScript
for
Beginners
```

----

splice() syntax:

array.splice(index, remove);   // Add new elements to an array

// "index" indicates the position to add elements

// "remove" specifies how many original elements should be removed.

e.g.

```
<script>
const arr = ["A", "B", "C", "D"];
arr.splice(2, 1, "10", "20", "30");
// add 3 elements at index 2, remove 1 original element "C"
document.write(arr);
</script>
// Output:   A,B,10,20,30,D
```

124

----

sqrt() syntax:

Math.sqrt();

// Return the square root of a number.

e.g.

<script>

var result = **Math.sqrt(25)**;

document.write (result);

</script>

// Output: 5

----

src syntax:

src="external.js"   // import an external Js script

src = "photo.jpg"   // load a image file

e.g.

<script **src="myScript.js"**></script>

// Import a specified external script "myScript.js" to the current html file.

e.g.

<html>

<img **src = "myPhoto.jpg"** width = "100" height = "80">

</html>

// Load an image "myPhoto.jpg" into the current html file.

----

static syntax:

Class.staticProperty

Class.staticMethod

// The static property and static method can be referenced by a class,
not by an object.

e.g.

```
<script>

class MyClass{

static greet() { return "Hello!"; }

static name = "Nancy";

}    // MyClass references the static method and the static property

document.write(MyClass.greet() +" ");

document.write(MyClass.name +" ");

</script>

// Output:   Hello!  Nancy
```

----

startsWith() syntax:

string.startsWith(searchvalue, start)

// Return true if a string begins with a specified value

// The startsWith() method is case sensitive.

e.g.

```
<script>

var str = "HTML CSS is very easy";

document.write(str.startsWith("HTML"));

</script>

// Output:   true
```

----

strict mode syntax:

// Strict Mode removes some JavaScript silent errors by altering them to throw exceptions or output nothing.

// To declare a Strict Mode, we can add a "use strict" at the beginning of the script.

e.g.

```
<script>

"use strict";   // using strict mode

num = 3.14;   // error! "num" is not declared, because it has no "var".
```

```
document.write("Result is: " + num);
</script>
```

// Output: nothing

e.g.

```
<script>     // do not use string mode
num = 3.14;    // OK !
document.write("Result is: " + num);
</script>
```

// Output: Result is 3.14

String() syntax:

String(parameter)

// Convert its parameter to a string.

e.g.

```
<script>
document.write(String(new Date()));   // convert to a string
</script>
```

// Output: Tue Sep 13 2022 12:50:38 GMT-0400

----

string length syntax:

string. length

// Calculate the string length, including spaces.

e.g.

```
<script>
var str = "I love JavaScript!";
var len = str.length;      // get the string length
document.write ( "String length is " + len );
</script>
```

// Output: String length is 18

----

string object syntax:

var object = new String("myString");

// Create a string object

e.g.

<script>

var person = new String("John");

document.write(person instanceof Object);   // check object

</script>

// Output: true

----

submit syntax:

<input type="submit" value="Submit">

// Submit the data in the form to the server

e.g.

<html>

<script language="javascript">

function send(){ alert ("Submit successfully!") }

</script>

<form name="myForm" >

User Name: <input type="text" name="user">

<input type="submit" value="Submit" onClick="send()">

</form>

</html>

// Output: Submit successfully!

----

submit() syntax:

form.submit()

// Submit the form data to the server.

e.g.

```
<html>

<form id="myform">

<textarea></textarea><br><br>

<input type="button" onClick="myfun()" value="submit" >

</form>

<script type="text/javascript">

function myfun() {

document.getElementById("myform").submit();

alert ("Data submitted successfully!");

}    // "submit( )" submits "myform" data to the server.

</script>

</html>

// Output:    Data submitted successfully!
```

----

substr() syntax:

string.substr(start, length);

// "substr(start, length)" can extract a substring from a string.

// "start" argument specifies the starting position to extract.

// "length" argument specifies the substring length.

e.g.

```
<script>

var str = "JavaScript is easy.";

var sub = str.substr( 4, 6 );  /* extract a substring from index 4, and
length 6.  */

document.write ( sub );

</script>

// Output:   Script
```

----

substring() syntax:

string.substring(start, end);

// "substring(start, end)" can extract a substring from a string.

// "start" argument specifies the starting position to extract.

// "end" argument specifies the ending position to extract.

e.g.

```
<script>
var str = "JavaScript is easy.";
var sub = str.substring( 4, 10 );   /* extract a substring from index 4 to index 10  */
document.write ( sub );
</script>
```

// Output: Script

----

super() syntax:

super(arg);

// "super()" is used to call the constructor of the base class

e.g.

```
<script>
class Person {    // base class
 constructor(name){this.name = name;}
 present(){
  return 'My name is ' + this.name;
 }
}
class Author extends Person {    // derived class
 constructor(name){super(name);}
}    // "super(name)" calls the constructor of the bass class
let obj = new Author("Ray Yao");
document.write(obj.present());
</script>
```

// Output: My name is Ray Yao

130

----

switch (var variable) {

 case 1: if equals this case, do this; **break;**

 case 2: if equals this case, do this; **break;**

 case 3: if equals this case, do this; **break;**

 default : if not equals any case, run default code; **break;**

 }

// The value of the variable will compare each case first, if equals one of the "case" value; it will execute that "case" code.

// "break;" ends the current statement.

e.g.

<script>

var number=20;

switch (number) { // number value compares each case

case 10 : document.write ("Running case 10"); break ;

case 20 : document.write ("Running case 20"); break;

case 30 : document.write ("Running case 30"); break;

default : document.write ("Running default code"); break; }

</script>

// Output: Running case 20

----

tan() syntax:

Math.tan(radian)

// Return the tangent value of a radian.

e.g.

<script>

document.write(**Math.tan(3.14)**);

</script>

// Output: -0.001592654936407223

131

----

test() syntax:

pattern.test("string")

// Checks whether a string matches a specified pattern, returning true if
the string contains matching text and false otherwise.

<script>

var patt = new RegExp("o");   // use regular expression

document.write(**patt.test("Hello")**); // check if the string contains "o"

</script>

// Output: true

----

this syntax:

this. property

this. method()

// "this" represents the current object

e.g.

<script>

house = new Object ( );   // create an object "house"

var size = "large";

var price = "expensive";

function build(){ return "good!" };

document.write ("House size: " + **this.size** + "<br>");

document.write ("House price: " + **this.price** + "<br>");

document.write ("House building: " + **this.build()** + "<br>");

</script>

// Output:

House size: large

House price: expensive

House building: good!

e.g.

```html
<html>
<button onclick="this.style.display='none'">Click Me!, I will be disappeared!</button>
</html>
```
// the button will disappear when it is clicked

// "this" represents the current object "button"

----

this.innerHTML syntax:

onclick="this.innerHTML='Text Changed!'"

// When the element is clicked, the contents will be changed

e.g.

```html
<html>
<h1 onclick="this.innerHTML='Text Changed!'">Click Me!</h1>
</html>
```

// Output: Text Changed!

----

throw syntax:

try { throw new Error();}   // throw exception

catch(e) { e.message }   // catch and process the exception

e.g.

```
<script>
try {
var x = 100, y =0;
if( x / y ) {
throw new Error('The y is 0');
}}
catch(e) {
document.write('An error caught<br>');
document.write('Error message: ' + e.message);
}    // "e.message" shows the exception message
```

```
</script>
```

// Output: An error caught

Error message: The y is 0

----

toExponential() syntax:

number.toExponential(length)

// Returns a number string in which numbers are rounded and written using exponential notation

e.g.

```
<script>
var num = 8.1688;
document.write(num.toExponential(4));
</script>
```

// Output: 8.1688e+0

----

toFixed() syntax:

Number.toFixed(decimalPlace);

// Convert a number into a string with the specified decimal place

e.g.

```
<script>
var num = 10.28;
var str = num.toFixed(1);     // 1 is decimal place
// convert the decimal number to string with 1 decimal place
document.write (str);
</script>
```

// Output: 10.3

----

toISOstring() syntax:

dateObject.toISOString()

// Convert a date to a ISO string

// ISO is the international standard of dates and times.

e.g.

```
<script>
const d = new Date();
document.write(d.toISOString());
</script>
// Output:   2022-09-20T20:42:38.739Z
```

----

tolowercase() syntax:

string.toLowerCase( )

// Convert the string to lower case.

e.g.

```
<script>
var str = "Hello World!";
var small = str.toLowerCase( );
document.write ( "Lowercase is " + small);
</script>
// Output:   Lowercase is hello world!
```

----

toPrecision() syntax:

number.toPrecision(length)

// Return a number string, with a specified length

e.g.

```
<script>
var num = 8.1688;
document.write(num.toPrecision(5));
</script>
// Output:   8.1688
```

----

toString() syntax:

array.toString();

// "array.toString()" converts a JavaScript array into a string.

e.g.

```
<script>
var myarray = new Array( );
myarray[0] ="Mon";
myarray[1] ="Tue";
myarray[2] ="Wed";
var days = myarray.toString( );   // convert to string
document.write ( days );
</script>
// Output:   Mon, Tue, Wed
```

----

toString() syntax:

number.toString( );

// "number.toString( )" can convert a number to a string.

e.g.

```
<script>
var num1 = 12; var num2 = 68;
var str1 = num1.toString( );     // convert to string
var str2 = num2.toString( );     // convert to string
var sum = str1 + str2;    // connecting instead of adding
document.write ( sum );
</script>
// Output:   1268
```

----

touppercase() syntax:

string.toUpperCase( )

// Convert the string to upper case

e.g.

```
<script>
var str = "Hello World!";
var big = str.toUpperCase( );
document.write ( "Uppercase is " + big);
</script>
// Output:   Uppercase is HELLO WORLD!
```

----

toUTCstring() syntax:

dateObject.toUTCString()

// Convert a date to a UTC string

// UTC (Universal Time Coordinated) is the same as GMT (Greenwich Mean Time).

e.g.

```
<script>
const d = new Date();
document.write(d.toUTCString());
</script>
// Output:   Tue, 20 Sep 2022 20:34:30 GMT
```

----

trim() syntax:

string.trim();

// Removes whitespace from both sides of a string

e.g.

```
<script>
var str1 = "    Hello World!     ";
var str2 = str1.trim();
document.write(str2);
</script>
// Output:   Hello World!
```

// The whitespaces of both sides of the string has been removed.

----

string.trimEnd();

// Removes whitespace from end side of a string

e.g.

```
<script>

var str1 = "    Hello World!    ";

var str2 = str1.trimEnd();

document.write(str2);

</script>
```

// Output: Hello World!

// The whitespaces of end side of the string has been removed.

----

string.trimStart();

// Removes whitespace from start side of a string

e.g.

```
<script>

var str1 = "    Hello World!    ";

var str2 = str1.trimStart();

document.write(str2);

</script>
```

// Output: Hello World!

// The whitespaces of start side of the string has been removed.

Math.trunc(number)

// Return the integer part of a number

e.g.

```
<script>
```

```
document.write(Math.trunc(123.456) + " ");

document.write(Math.trunc(-123.456) + " ");

</script>
```

// Output: 123   -123

<h3 align="center">try…catch…finally syntax:</h3>

try { // exception code }   // throw exception

catch(e) { // e.message }   // catch and process exception

finally { // must run }   // finally execute

e.g.

```
<script>

const x= 100, y = 200;

try { document.write(num);}

catch(e) {

document.write("Error message: " + e.message +"<br>");

}    // "e.message" shows the exception message

finally {document.write("Exception occurs!");}

</script>
```

// Output: Error message: num is not defined

Exception occurs!

<h3 align="center">typeOf syntax:</h3>

typeof operand

// Return the type of the operand

e.g.

```
<script>

const num = 10;

document.write(typeof num +" ");

document.write(typeof 'hello' +" ");

document.write(typeof true +" ");
```

```
document.write(typeof null +" ");

document.write(typeof x +" ");

</script>
```

// Output: number   string   Boolean   object   undefined

----

undefined syntax:

undefined

// If a variable has not assigned any value, then it is called undefined.

e.g.

```
<script>
```

let myVariable;

```
document.write(typeof myVariable);

</script>
```

// Output: undefined

----

unshift() syntax:

array.unshift();

// Add one or more elements in the beginning of an array.

e.g.

```
<script>

var arr = [4,5,6];
```

arr.unshift(1,2,3);   // add 1,2,3 to the beginning of "arr"

```
document.write (arr);

</script>
```

// Output: 1,2,3,4,5,6

----

validity.rangeOverflow syntax:

document.getElementById("myform").validity.rangeOverflow

// Return true if the element value too large

e.g.

```html
<html>
<input id="fm" type="number" max="100">
<button onclick="myFun()">Check</button>
<script>
function myFun() {
var num = "";    // please input a number less than or equal to 100
   if (document.getElementById("fm").validity.rangeOverflow) {
      num = "The number is too larger!";
   } else {
      num = "Correct Input";
   }
   document.write(num);
}
</script>
</html>
// Correct Input!
```

----

validity.rangeUnderflow syntax:

document.getElementById("myform").validity.rangeUnderflow

```
// Return true if the element value too small
```

e.g.

```html
<html>
<input id="fm" type="number" min="100">
<button onclick="myFun()">Check</button>
<script>
function myFun() {
var num = "";    // please input a number greater than or equal to 100
   if (document.getElementById("fm").validity.rangeUnderflow) {
      num = "The number is too small!";
   } else {
```

```
        num = "Correct Input";

    }

    document.write(num);

}

</script>

</html>

// Correct Input!
```

----

valueOf() syntax:

object.value()

```
// Return the primitive value of a number object

// Return the primitive value of a string object

// Return the primitive value of an array object

e.g.

<script>

var num = new Number(123);

var str = new String("hello");

var arr = ["apple", "banana", "cherry"];

document.write(num.valueOf()+" "+str.valueOf()+" "+arr.valueOf());

</script>

// Output:  123    hello    apple, banana, cherry
```

----

variable syntax:

var variable_name = value;

```
// JavaScript variable uses "var" to define

e.g.

<script type = "text/javascript">

var abcde=100;     // define a variable "abcde"

var abc888="Hello World";     // define a variable "abc888"

var my_variable=true;     // define a variable "my_variable"
```

```
</script>
```

---

void() syntax:

javascript:void()

// "void()" can evaluate an expression, but does not return any value.

e.g.

```
<a href="javascript:void(document.write("Hello"))">Click Me</a>
```

// Output: Hello

e.g.

```
<a href="javascript:void(0)">Click me. Nothing happen!</a>
```

// Output: Click me. Nothing happen!

---

web worker syntax:

let obj = new Worker("external_file.js");

// The web worker works as a background application.

obj.terminate();   // terminate the web worker

e.g.

```
<script>
```

let w = new Worker("background.js"); // create a web worker

w.terminate();   // terminate the web worker

```
</script>
```

// Result: (Web Worker runs in background, not affect the page)

---

while loop syntax:

while (test-expression) { // some js code in here; **}**

// "while loop" loops through a block of code if the specified condition is true.

e.g.

```
<script>
var counter=0;
```

143

```
while (counter < 8) {    // loop 8 times
document.write ( "&" );
counter++;     // increase 1 every loop
}
</script>
// Output:   &&&&&&&&
```

----

with syntax:

with (object){ properties }

with (object){ methods }

```
// "with" keyword is used as a shorthand for an object to reference
property or method.
// Namely one object references multiple properties or methods.
// Do not use "with" in strict mode.
e.g.
<script>
```

with (Math) {   // using "Math"

```
document.write(round(10.5) + " ");  // Math references round()
document.write(max(10.5, 9) + " ");  // Math references max()
document.write(min(10.5, 9) + " ");  // Math references min()
}
</script>
// Output:   11   10.5    9
```

Appendix

JavaScript Keywords Chart

abstract	arguments	await	boolean
break	byte	case	catch
char	class	const	continue
debugger	default	delete	do
double	else	enum	eval
export	extends	false	final
finally	float	for	function
goto	if	implements	import
in	instanceof	int	interface
let	long	native	new
null	package	private	protected
public	return	short	static
super	switch	synchronized	this
throw	throws	transient	true
try	typeof	var	void
volatile	while	with	yield

Escape Chart

Escape	Output
\'	Single quotes
\"	Double quotation marks
\\	The backslash
\n	A newline
\r	Enter
\t	Horizontal Tabulator
\b	Back space
\f	Page identifier
\v	Vertical Tabulator

String Properties Chart

Property	Describe
constructor	Returns a function that creates a string attribute
length	Returns the length of the string
prototype	Allows to add properties, methods to an object

Data Types Chart

Types	Description
string	a character or a string of characters
number	an integer or floating point number
boolean	a value with true or false.
function	a user-defined method
object	a built-in or user-defined object

String Methods Chart

Method	Describe
charAt()	Returns the character at the specified index
charCodeAt()	Returns a character Unicode at specified index
concat()	Concatenates two or more strings
fromCharCode()	Convert Unicode to a string
indexOf()	Returns the first specified character index in a string
lastIndexOf()	Returns the last specified character index in a string
localeCompare()	Compare two strings in a locally specific order
match()	Find a match for one or more regular expressions
replace()	Replaces the substring that matches regular expression
search()	Retrieves the value that matches regular expression
slice()	Return the extracted part in a string
split()	Split a string into an array of substrings
substr()	Extracts a specified number of characters in a string.
substring()	Extract characters in string between two specified indexes
toLowerCase()	Convert a string to lowercase
toString()	Returns the string object value
toUpperCase()	Convert a string to uppercase
trim()	Removes whitespace at the beginning and end of a string
valueOf()	Returns the original value of a string object

Arithmetic Operators Chart

Operator	description	Example	Result
+	add	result=5+2	7
-	subtract	result=5-2	3
*	multiply	result=5*2	10
**	exponentiate	result=5**2	25
/	divide	result=5/2	2.5
%	remainder	result=5%2	1
++	increase	result=++5	6
++	increase	result=5++	5
--	decrease	result=--5	4
--	decrease	result=5--	5

Assignment Operators Chart   Given a = 10, y = 5

Operators	Examples	Equals	Results
+=	a+=b	a=a+b	a=15
-=	a-=b	a=a-b	a=5
*=	a*=b	a=a*b	a=50
**=	a **=b	a=a**b	a=100000
/=	a/=b	a=a/b	a=2
%=	a%=b	a=a%b	a=0

Comparison Operators Chart   (Given n = 5)

Oprt	Descriptions	Compare	Return
==	equal to	n==8	false
===	(type & value) equal to	n==="5"	false
!=	not equal to	n!=8	true
!==	(type & value) not equal to	n!=="5"	true
>	greater than	n>8	false
<	less than	n<8	true
>=	greater than or equal to	n>=8	false
<=	less than or equal to	n<=8	true

Logical Operators Chart   (Given a = 6, b = 3)

Oprt	Description	Examples
&&	and	(a < 10 && b > 1) // true
||	or	(a==5 || b==5) // false
!	not	!(a==b) // true

Type Operators Chart

Oprt	Description
typeof	get the type of a variable
instanceof	get true if an object is an instance of an object

Bitwise Operators Chart

Oprt	Evaluate	Example	Binary	Result
&	and	5 & 1	0101 & 0001	0001
|	or	5 | 1	0101 | 0001	0101
~	not	~ 5	~0101	1010
^	xor	5 ^ 1	0101 ^ 0001	0100
<<	left shift	5 << 1	0101 << 1	1010
>>	right shift	5 >> 1	0101 >> 1	0010
>>>	right shift	5 >>> 1	0101 >>> 1	0010

Note: >>> is unsigned right shift

Logical Assignment Operators Chart

Operator	Example	Same As
&=	a &= b	a = a & b
^=	a ^= b	a = a ^ b
|=	a |= b	a = a | b

Shift Assignment Operators Chart

Operator	Example	Same As
<<=	a <<= b	a = a << b
>>=	a >>= b	a = a >> b
>>>=	a >>>= b	a = a >>> b

Logical Operation Chart

true && true; returns true;	true && false; returns false;	false &&false; returns false;
true II true; returns true;	true II false; returns true;	false II false; return false;
! false; returns true;	! true; returns false;	

JavaScript Errors Chart

Errors Thrown	Description
EvalError	An error in the eval() function has occurred
RangeError	A number "out of range" has occurred
ReferenceError	An illegal reference has occurred
SyntaxError	A syntax error has occurred
TypeError	A type error has occurred
URIError	An error in encodeURI() has occurred

Dom Element Finding Chart

Dom Method	Description
document.getElementById(id)	Find an element by element id
document.getElementsByTagName(name)	Find elements by tag name
document.getElementsByClassName(name)	Find elements by class name

Date Get Methods Chart

Methods	Descriptions
getDate()	Get a date of the month (1 to 31).
getDay()	Get a day of the week (0 to 6).
getFullYear()	Get the year in four digits.
getHours()	Get the hour (0 to 23).
getMilliseconds()	Get the milliseconds (0 to 999).
getMinutes()	Get the minutes (0 to 59).
getMonth()	Get the month (0 to 11).
getSeconds()	Get the number of seconds (0 to 59).
getTime()	Get the milliseconds since January 1, 1970.

Date Set Methods Chart

Method	Description
setDate()	Set the day as a number (1-31)
setFullYear()	Set the year (optionally month and day)
setHours()	Set the hour (0-23)
setMilliseconds()	Set the milliseconds (0-999)
setMinutes()	Set the minutes (0-59)
setMonth()	Set the month (0-11)
setSeconds()	Set the seconds (0-59)
setTime()	Set the time (milliseconds since January 1, 1970)

Date Format Chart

Type	Example
ISO Date	"2022-06-18" (International Standard Organization)
Short Date	"06/18/2022"
Long Date	"Jun 18 2022" or "18 Jun 2022"

Constraint Validation of Html Chart

Property	Description
disabled	Specifies that the input element is not available
max	Specifies the maximum value of the input element
min	Specifies the minimum value of the input element
pattern	Specifies the pattern for input element values
required	Specifies that input element fields are required
type	Specifies the type of the input element

Constrain Validation of Css Chart

Selector	Description
:disabled	Select the input element whose attribute is "disabled"
:invalid	Select an invalid input element
:optional	Select the input element without "optional" attribute
:required	Select the input element with the "required" attribute
:valid	Selects the input elements with valid values

Constraint Validation of Dom Chart

Validity	Description
checkValidity()	Return true if the data in the input element is valid
setCustomValidity()	Set a method for customizing error messages.
validity	Return true if the input value is valid
validationMessage	Display the browser error message
willValidate	Specify whether the input requires a validation

Validity Properties Chart

Propery	Description
customError	Set to true if the user-defined validity information is set, or if a custom validity message is set.
patternMismatch	Set to true if the element's value does not match its pattern attribute.
rangeOverflow	Set to true if the value of the element is greater than the maximum value.
rangeUnderflow	Set to true if the value of the element is less than the minimum value.
stepMismatch	Set to true if the element's value is not set according to the specified step attribute.
tooLong	Set to true if the value of the element exceeds the length set by the maxLength attribute.
typeMismatch	Set to true if the element's value is not the type expected to match.
valueMissing	Set to true if the element with "required" attribute has no value.
valid	Set to true if the element's value is valid, which means False if the element's value is invalid.

Event Chart

Event	Happen
onabort	when the image is stopped loading by user
onblur	when the element loses fours
onchange	when the content of an element has been changed
onclick	when the element is clicked
ondragdrop	when a file is dragged and drop into the browser window
onerror	when an error occurs
onfocus	when the element is focused
onkeydown	when the key is down
onkeypress	when the key is pressed
onkeyup	when the key is up
onload	when the page has been loaded
onmessage	when a message is received from an event source
onmouseout	when the mouse is moved out of an element
onmouseover	when the mouse is moved over an element
onmouseup	when the mouse is up
onreset	when the data in the form is reset
onresize	when the size of the browser window is changed
onselect	when the text in the textarea is selected
onsubmit	when the form data is submitted

Number Properties Chart

Properties	Descriptions
Number.MAX_VALUE	The maximum value
Number.MIN_VALUE	The minimum value
Number.NaN	Not a number
Number.NEGATIVE_INFINITY	-infinity, returns on overflow
Number.POSITIVE_INFINITY	+infinity, returns on overflow
Number.MIN_SAFE_INTEGER	Minimum safe integer.
Number.MAX_SAFE_INTEGER	Maximum safe integer.

Number Methods Chart

Methods	Descriptions
Number.parseFloat()	Convert a string to a floating point number,
Number.parseInt()	Convert a string to an integer number,
Number.isFinite()	Check if the parameter is a finite number.
Number.isInteger()	Check if the parameter is an integer.
Number.isNaN()	Check if the parameter is NaN
toExponential()	Gets a string of an exponential number
toFixed()	Gets a number with specified decimal places
toPrecision()	Gets a number of the specified precision.

Json Functions Chart

Function	Description
JSON.parse()	Convert Json string to JavaScript value
JSON.stringify()	Convert JavaScript value to Json String

Regular Expression Chart

RegExp	Description
i	Perform case-insensitive matching.
g	Perform global matching
m	Perform multiple line matching.
[abc]	Find any character between square brackets.
[0-9]	Find any number from 0 to 9.
(x|y)	Find any options using |.
\d	Match numbers.
\s	Match whitespace characters.
\b	Match word boundaries.
n+	Match any string containing at least one n.
n*	Match any string containing zero or more n's.
n?	Match any string containing zero or one n.

Css Selectors Chart

Selector	Description
:disabled	Select the input element whose attribute is "disabled"
:invalid	Select an invalid input element
:optional	Select the input element without "optional" attribute
:required	Select the input element with the "required" attribute
:valid	Selects the input elements with valid values

Math Methods Chart (1)

Method	Description
abs(num)	Get the absolute value of num
acos(num)	Get the arccosine of num in radians
acosh(num)	Get the hyperbolic arccosine of num
asin(num)	Get the arcsine of num in radians
asinh(num)	Get the hyperbolic arcsine of num
atan(num)	Get the arctangent of num between-PI/2 and PI/2 radians
atan2(num, n)	Get the arctangent of the quotient of its arguments
atanh(num)	Get the hyperbolic arctangent of num
cbrt(num)	Get the cubic root of num
ceil(num)	Get num rounded upwards to the nearest integer
cos(num)	Get the cosine of num (num is in radians)
cosh(num)	Get the hyperbolic cosine of num
exp(num)	Get the value of Ex
floor(num)	Get num rounded downwards to the nearest integer
log(num)	Get the natural logarithm (base E) of num
max(n1, n2...)	Get the number with the highest value
min(n1, n2...)	Get the number with the lowest value
pow(num, n)	Get the value of num to the power of n
random()	Get a random number between 0 and 1
round(num)	Get a rounded num to the nearest integer
sign(num)	Get if num is negative, null or positive (-1, 0, 1)
sin(num)	Get the sine of num (num is in radians)
sinh(num)	Get the hyperbolic sine of num

Math Methods Chart (2)

Method	Description
sqrt(num)	Get the square root of num
tan(num)	Get the tangent of an angle number
tanh(num)	Get the hyperbolic tangent of a number
trunc(num)	Get the integer part of the num
log(num)	Get the natural logarithm (base E) of num

Cookie Chart

Create or modify a cookie document.cookie = "name=xxx; expires=date";
Read a cookie let variable = document.cookie;
Delete a cookie document.cookie = "name=xxx; expires=date; path=/;";

Note: To delete a cookie, just set the expire parameter to a past date.

Set Collection Chart

Set	Description
new Set()	Creates a new Set
add()	Adds a new element to the Set
delete()	Removes an element from a Set
has()	Returns true if a value exists
clear()	Removes all elements from a Set
forEach()	Invokes a callback for each element
values()	Get an Iterator with all the values in a Set
keys()	Same as values()
entries()	Get an Iterator with value/value pairs in a Set
size	Get the number of elements in a Set

Map Collection Chart

Map	Description
new Map()	Creates a new Map object
set()	Sets the value for a key in a Map
get()	Gets the value for a key in a Map
clear()	Removes all the elements from a Map
delete()	Removes a Map element specified by a key
has()	Return true if a key exists in a Map
forEach()	Invokes a callback for each key/value pair in a Map
entries()	Get an iterator object with key/value pairs in a Map
keys()	Get an iterator object with the keys in a Map
values()	Get an iterator object of the values in a Map
size	Get the number of elements in a Map

And Bitwise Chart

Evaluation	Result	Examples	Result
0 & 0	0	1111 & 0000	0000
0 & 1	0	1111 & 0001	0001
1 & 0	0	1111 & 0010	0010
1 & 1	1	1111 & 0100	0100

Or Bitwise Chart

Evaluation	Result	Examples	Result
0 | 0	0	1111 | 0000	1111
0 | 1	1	1111 | 0001	1111
1 | 0	1	1111 | 0010	1111
1 | 1	1	1111 | 0100	1111

Xor Bitwise Chart

Evaluation	Result	Examples	Result
0 ^ 0	0	1111 ^ 0000	1111
0 ^ 1	1	1111 ^ 0001	1110
1 ^ 0	1	1111 ^ 0010	1101
1 ^ 1	0	1111 ^ 0100	1011

Dom Changing Element Chart

Dom Property & Method	Description
element.innerHTML = new html content	Change the inner Html content of an Html element
element.attribute = new value	Change the attribute value of an Html element
element.style.property = new style	Change the style property of an Html element
element.setAttribute(attribute, value)	Change the attribute value of an Html element

Dom Adding & Deleting Element Chart

Dom Method	Description
document.createElement(element)	Create an HTML element
document.removeChild(element)	Remove an HTML element
document.appendChild(element)	Add an HTML element
document.replaceChild(new, old)	Replace an HTML element
document.write(text)	Write into the HTML output stream

Class Method & Keywords Chart

constructor()	Create and initialize a class
extends	Inherit a class
static	Define a static method in a class
super	Call the constructor of the parent class

Document Property Chart

Property	Returns
document.anchors	get all <a> elements with name attribute
document.baseURI	get the base URI of the document
document.body	get the <body> element
document.cookie	get the document's cookie
document.doctype	get the document's doctype
document.documentElement	get the <html> element
document.documentMode	get the mode used by the browser
document.documentURI	get the URI of the document
document.domain	get the domain name of the server
document.embeds	get all <embed> elements
document.forms	get all <form> elements
document.head	get the <head> element
document.images	get all <img> elements
document.implementation	get the DOM implementation
document.inputEncoding	get the document's encoding
document.lastModified	get the date time of document updated
document.links	get all <area> & <a> with href attributes
document.readyState	get the loading status of the document
document.referrer	get the URI of the referrer
document.scripts	get all <script> elements
document.strictErrorChecking	Returns if error checking is enforced
document.title	Returns the <title> element
document.URL	Returns the complete URL of the document

Node Accessing Chart

Property	Description
parentNode	Access the parent node
childNodes[index]	Access the child nodes
firstChild	Access the first child node
lastChild	Access the last child node
nextSibling	Access the next sibling node
previousSibling	Access the previous sibling node
nodeName	Access the node name
nodeType	Access the node type
nodeValue	Access the node value

Window Method & Property Chart

Methods	Descriptions
window.open()	open a new window
window.close()	close the current window
window.moveTo()	move the current window
window.resizeTo()	resize the current window
window.open()	open a new window
window.close()	close the current window
window.moveTo()	move the current window
window.resizeTo()	resize the current window
window.localStorage	allow to store the data without expiration date
window.sessionStorage	allow to store the data for one session

Window Screen Chart

Property	Description
window.screen.width	get the screen width
window.screen.height	get the screen height
window.screen.availWidth	get the screen available width
window.screen.availHeight	get the screen available height
window.screen.colorDepth	get the screen color depth
window.screen.pixelDepth	get the screen pixel depth

Window Location Chart

Property	Description
window.location.href	get the href url of the current page
window.location.hostname	get the domain name of web host
window.location.pathname	get the path and filename
window.location.protocol	get the http:// or https:// protocol
window.location.assign()	get a new document

Window Navigator Chart

Property	Description
window.navigator.cookieEnabled	return true if cookies are enabled
window.navigator.appCodeName	return the browser name
window.navigator.platform	return the browser platform
window.navigator.appName	return the browser code name
window.navigator.product	return the product name of browser
window.navigator.appVersion	return the browser version
window.navigator.userAgent	return the user agent of the browser
window.navigator.language	return the browser's language
window.navigator.online	return true if the browser is online
window.navigator.javaEnabled	return true if Java is enabled

Storage Object Chart

Property/Method	Description
key(n)	Get the name of the nth key in the storage
length	Get the number of data items stored in the storage
getItem(key)	Get the value of the specified key name
setItem(key, value)	Add a key to the storage, or updates a key value
removeItem(key)	Remove that key from the storage
clear()	Clear all key out of the storage

Paperback Books by Ray Yao

Advanced C++ in 8 Hours

Advanced Java in 8 Hours

AngularJs in 8 Hours

C# Examination

C# Examples

C# Programming

C# Cheat Sheet

C++ Examination

C++ Examples

C++ Programming

C++ Cheat Sheet

Dart in 8 Hours

Django in 8 Hours

Erlang in 8 Hours

Git Github in 8 Hours

Go in 8 Hours

Google Sheet in 8 Hours

Haskell in 8 Hours

Html Css Examination

Html Css Examples

Html Css Programming

Html Css Cheat Sheet

Java Examination

Java Examples

Java Programming

Java Cheat Sheet

JavaScript Examination

JavaScript Examples

JavaScript Programming

JavaScript Cheat Sheet

JQuery Examination

JQuery Programming

Kotlin in 8 Hours

Linux Command Line

Linux Examination

Lua in 8 Hours

Matlab in 8 Hours

Matplotlib in 8 Hours

MySql Programming

Node.Js in 8 Hours

NumPy in 8 Hours

Pandas in 8 Hours

Perl in 8 Hours

Php MySql Examination

Php MySql Examples

Php MySql Programming

Php MySql Cheat Sheet

PowerShell in 8 Hours

Python Examination

Python Examples

Python Programming

Python Cheat Sheet

R Programming

React.Js in 8 Hours

Ruby Programming

Rust in 8 Hours

Scala in 8 Hours

Shell Scripting in 8 Hours

Swift in 8 Hours

TypeScript in 8 Hours

Visual Basic Examination

Visual Basic Programming

Vue.Js in 8 Hours

Xml Json in 8 Hours

Paperback Books by Ray Yao

C# Examination

C# Examples

C++ Examination

C++ Examples

Html Css Examination

Html Css Examples

Java Examination

Java Examples

JavaScript Examination

JavaScript Examples

JQuery Examination

JQuery Examples

Php MySql Examination

Php MySql Examples

Python Examination

Python Examples

Paperback Books by Ray Yao

C# Cheat Sheet

C++ Cheat Sheet

JAVA Cheat Sheet

JavaScript Cheat Sheet

PHP MySQL Cheat Sheet

Python Cheat Sheet

Html Css Cheat Sheet

Linux Command Line

Printed in Great Britain
by Amazon

19335756R00099